Old Habits Die Hard:

A Convent Mystery

SUSAN MATTERN

Sibylline Press

Copyright © 2025 by Susan Mattern
All Rights Reserved.

Published in the United States by Sibylline Press,
an imprint of All Things Book LLC, California.

Sibylline Press is dedicated to publishing the
brilliant work of women authors ages 50 and older.
www.sibyllinepress.com

Sibylline Digital First Edition
eBook ISBN: 9798897409839
Print ISBN: 9798897409846
Library of Congress Control Number: 2025938568

Cover Design: Alicia Feltman
Book Production: Aaron Laughlin

HUMAN AUTHORED: Any use of this publication to train generative artificial intelligence (AI) technologies to generate text is expressly prohibited

Sibylline
Press

CONVENT MYSTERY #4

HOT CHOCOLATE

CHAPTER 1

November, 1970

I was finally moving into David's apartment. It was so much nicer than mine, overlooking the Mississippi River from six stories high. I could spend hours looking out the huge picture window in his living room and watch the barges and tugboats on the river.

It had been years since I first met David at the motherhouse during that first murder Inez and I tried to solve. I ended up getting kicked out of the convent, but it turned out to be the best thing that had ever happened to me in my short life. Falling in love with David was like a dream come true. Although I wasn't ready for marriage yet, I was ready to live with him and experience things I had only read about in books. Books I couldn't read in the convent, but that I guiltily read after I left. I had a lot of leftover guilt from the convent and the church.

I had paid the next month's rent in advance for my old apartment, so I had a few extra weeks to move out. It was a Tuesday afternoon and I sat in my bedroom, going through old papers and music I had collected during my years at Washington University. I didn't need to bring all of it, and this was the perfect time for some cleaning.

As I went through my extensive collection of music, I discovered some organ pieces that belonged to Sister Anne. She was a nun I'd met at a music festival who was three years older than me. She belonged to a smaller congregation, Our Lady of Perpetual Help. She had lent me some Bach pieces for the organ and piano. We intended to keep in touch but never did. I felt terrible that I had never returned them, but I remembered she was stationed at a parish in Kirkwood, not too far from where I lived. I got up and looked through the phone book for St. Boniface parish and convent in Kirkwood. I might as well call now and see if she was still there.

"Hello, I'd like to speak with Sister Anne."

"Of course. Let me check and see if she's home."

I waited a few minutes.

The sister returned to the line. "Who is this? Can I have your number? When she gets home, I'll have her call you."

I explained who I was and thanked her.

I carefully separated all the music I intended to keep from what I planned to donate. Just as I was finishing up, the phone rang.

"Hello."

"Hello, this is Sister Anne. Someone named Kristen called me from this number?"

"Hi, this is Kristen Byrne. I met you at that music festival a few years ago, and you lent me some of your music. I never got it back to you."

"Oh, I remember you. You played the piano so beautifully."

"And I was so impressed with how wonderfully you played the organ. The music you lent me was mostly Bach pieces for keyboard. I hope I can still return them."

"I totally forgot about that, but it would be great to get them back. And I'd love to see you again. How are you?"

We chatted for a while. Sister Anne told me she usually practiced every day from three to four at the church and invited me to stop by any time so we could catch up on our lives.

"I'll definitely come by this week."

★ ★ ★

When David came home that night, I had dinner prepared for him. I didn't want to assume the role of housewife and cook—that was *not* who I was—but I did enjoy cooking for two sometimes. We sat down at the dining-room table overlooking the beautiful view of the city from his sixth-floor apartment.

He took a bite of pasta. "Do you realize that in the three years I've known you, we've investigated three convent-related murders? That's hard to believe. I'm glad I've settled back into a life of petty theft, fraud, and Mafia dealings in South St. Louis. It's much more enjoyable and fulfilling."

I laughed. "Yep, no more convent murders. All my friends have graduated and are out on mission, and I'm not in touch with any of them anymore, except Pam, and she left too, so we're done with convent murders. And no more Sister Inez, either. Thank God. I did like her as a person, though. One of my many mistakes about judging people's characters. Although I do have to return some music to a sister this week. She's still in a convent in Kirkwood."

"Well, that's fine. Just make sure she doesn't get killed. Or if she does, make sure you aren't around when it happens!"

It truly wasn't a laughing matter, and we both knew it, but it was extremely strange that I had been involved in all three murders. Not that my interference had accomplished anything. I'd almost gotten myself killed during the first murder investigation, and JC, my cat, had helped solve the second one. The third murderer was caught because of a lost piece of jewelry. I had been less than helpful in all three investigations, and I hoped to never set foot in another convent as long as I lived. I attended church occasionally, but not every week, and certainly not every day like I used to when I was a nun.

I liked my spiritual life right now, just the way it was—or wasn't.

"Don't worry. I'm never setting foot in a convent again. And I'm never talking to a priest again—or a nun. Well, except for this one last time. I'll go into the church, give Sister Anne the music, listen to her play, catch up a bit, and then that's it."

"Promise?"

"Yes, I promise."

"On the Bible?"

"Oh, my God. Don't be so melodramatic. How about I swear on my old rule book? That's even better. You know I still have it, as well as my old habit. I can always wear it."

David laughed. "I love what you're wearing now. It's quite an improvement, trust me."

"Some Halloween, if I can still fit into the habit, I'll dress up as a nun. Maybe a few years from now."

★ ★ ★

On Thursday, I drove to St. Boniface after class with about ten pieces of music. The church had been modern in 1947, but two decades later, it had begun to look shabby and outdated. The soaring aluminum arches didn't match the traditional stained glass beneath them, and the whole church was a clash of medieval and contemporary styles that didn't fit well together. I parked my car and walked inside. For all the stained glass and large windows, it was gloomy and cold. And silent. I didn't hear anyone playing, even though there was a light on in the choir loft. I wondered if Anne was still up there practicing.

I sat in the back pew, waiting a few minutes to decide what to do. I could go over to the convent, even though I hated the idea. No, I would just wait; after all, I had promised. Then I heard a voice coming from the choir loft.

"Just get out. No, I mean it. Get out. Don't come up here again."

Then, a bang, like someone had thrown a book or dropped something on the floor. Then loud footsteps. A few minutes later, a door slammed behind me, but I didn't look around. There must have been two entrances to the choir loft, and someone came down the other staircase, farther from me, and went outside.

I finally heard the organ. It was Bach. It had to be Anne playing. I walked to the nearest choir door and climbed the steps. I knocked even though she probably couldn't hear me and opened the door at the top of the stairs. When Anne saw me, she stopped playing.

"Kristen?" She stood quickly and walked over to me.

"It's so good to see you." She hugged me.

"It's great to see you too." I noticed her eyes were red. "Are you okay? I heard some yelling up here."

"Oh, I'm sorry you heard that. It was nothing. Nothing to worry about."

I handed her the music. "I'm sorry I kept it for so long."

"That's fine. It gives us a chance to reconnect after all these years. Here, sit down."

I sat down on one of the hard wooden pews. "Why don't you play a little more of that gorgeous Bach, and then we can go somewhere and talk?"

"That sounds wonderful. I'm tired of practicing anyway. There's a Walgreens in the next block. We can get a drink there. I'd love to catch up and hear what you've been doing."

Anne played the piece she had started to practice when I came in. She was an excellent organist. I was better at the piano. I didn't have the patience for all those organ pedals. The piece was beautiful, but when she was finished, she put her music away. We headed out through the big wooden doors and down the street to the corner drugstore. We both ordered hot chocolate.

"I need a treat today," she said.

"You sound like you might."

"But first, tell me about you since you left."

I told her about all my many adventures since getting kicked out of the convent, ending with moving in with David.

She asked all the right questions and appeared genuinely interested. She couldn't believe I had been involved in investigating so many murders. And she was intrigued by my relationship with David.

I had always admired Anne from a distance, even though I had never even spoken more than a few words to her during that conversation when we exchanged some music.

"What's life like out on mission?" I was curious.

"It's okay. Do you mind if I tell you something?"

"Not at all. I'm not going to tell anyone. I don't speak to anyone in the convent anymore. In fact, I promised David you would be the last sister I ever talked with."

"Well, I don't want you to break that promise." She was quiet for a minute. "Mission isn't exactly what I thought it would be."

"What do you mean?"

"I'm a lot freer, and I love that. I hated all the rules and regulations of our motherhouse, but it's hard to make friends here. There aren't enough people to choose from. There weren't many people in the motherhouse either, but at least they were around my same age. I have made a good friend, but she's not even a sister. She's the mother of one of my students, and we meet for coffee every once in a while. I don't really have any other friends."

"Wow, I'm sorry. You must be lonely."

"Yeah, I am. But I like teaching and I love to practice. You should come out here and play our piano in the convent. It's a beautiful Steinway. "

"Where did you get a Steinway?" I asked, envious.

"A woman from the parish gave it to us last year. She didn't have any children and couldn't play anymore because of arthritis, so she donated it to the convent. They planned to place it in the church, but it was too large to fit by the altar, so we put it in our sitting room instead. Why don't you come over next week to play it? I'd love to hear you play."

There went my promise, right out the window. I couldn't pass up the opportunity to play a beautiful Steinway. That was on my bucket list, and now I had the chance. Sorry, David.

"I'd love to come. When's a good time?"

"How about next Thursday at the same time? We'll skip the hot chocolate unless we get tired of playing and decide to come down here anyway." She glanced at her watch. "I'd better get going. I don't want to be late for prayers. I'm usually late, and I'd better start being good."

I laughed. I knew the feeling of trying to be good, even though you didn't really mean it. We said goodbye and hugged.

"See you next week," I said. "And thanks for the invitation. I'm looking forward to it."

★ ★ ★

I shared all the details of the visit with David.

"That was a quickly broken promise," he said with a smile.

"I know, but I would truly love to see and play that piano. It sounds amazing. If it turns out to be terrible, I'll come straight home."

"I'm only kidding. Stay as long as you want. Especially if you have a gourmet dinner ready for me when I get home from work."

I hit his arm. "Like that's going to happen. Steak and Shake is right down the street. Remember?"

"Oh, yeah, how could I forget? Our second home. We're like family to them."

I laughed. "I can't imagine a better family to have. They love us, and we love them!"

★ ★ ★

As I stood in front of the brick convent the following Thursday, I realized again how glad I was that I had gotten kicked out of my convent a few years earlier. I could have ended up in a place like this for my entire life.

The building stood two stories tall. Its style resembled the contemporary church across the parking lot, featuring soaring glass windows with steel framing that was already rusting. The glass was plain, and the entire structure appeared more like an office building than a church.

"Yes?" An elderly nun, her face wrinkled with a sad-looking expression, looked at me as I walked in. "Oh, oh, come in, come in."

For all the sleek lines on the building's exterior, its interior resembled a funeral parlor in its dreariness. The tile floor featured the black-and-white checkered pattern commonly found in public bathrooms, and the corridor was narrow and dimly lit.

"Please, come sit in the parlor. Would you like some tea? I'm Sister Frances."

"No, thank you, Sister. I'd like to speak with Sister Anne."

"Yes, she knows you're coming. I'll get her right away."

Sister Frances walked quickly for someone her age and weight. I figured she was in her seventies and probably weighed well over two hundred pounds, yet she was surprisingly light on her feet. She disappeared out the door and reappeared a few minutes later, followed by Sister Anne.

Anne led me to the room that held the Steinway.

The piano was beautiful, in tune, and likely built in the '40s. Steinways could last forever if properly cared for. This piano was a large grand with a massive sound that filled the room. I had come prepared with a folder of my favorite music. Anne and I sat and played for over an hour, talking and laughing the entire time. We made plans to perform duets, concerts, and a Christmas program—the works. Eventually, when we grew tired of practicing, we returned to Walgreens.

Anne ordered hot chocolate again along with a cookie, while I chose an iced tea and a chocolate-chip cookie that I couldn't resist.

"So, how are you feeling this week?" I asked when our snack arrived. "Are things any better?"

Anne put down her cup and cookie and looked at me. "I need to tell you something. I don't have anyone else to talk to. I feel like I can trust you, even though I've only known you for a couple of weeks. Well, a week, actually."

"Of course. You can share anything with me. After all, I'm the person who was kicked out of the convent for accusing a priest of murder. I'm not in any position to judge anyone about anything."

"Well, I'm probably going to leave right after Christmas."

"Oh, I'm sorry. I thought you might be leaving, after what you said last week about not being able to make any friends. It can get very lonely, I imagine, out on mission. But that's just in a few months. Can't you wait until the end of the school year? What will you do for a job?"

"I can't wait. I'm pregnant."

"Oh." I wasn't sure what to say next.

"Are you shocked?"

"No, I'm not shocked. Well—maybe a little. But mostly I'm worried about you and what you're going to do. Do you have a place to go?"

"The father of the baby can't get away right now, but he plans to come and be with me next year after I have the baby, to support us. We'll get married and become a regular family as soon as we can."

"Are you sure he's going to do that?"

"Yes, I trust him completely. I know that may sound naïve, but I believe he's telling the truth."

"Where will you go in the meantime?"

"My parents said I could come and stay with them."

"Who's the father?"

"I haven't told anyone who he is, and I can't, but I trust him completely and know he'll do the right thing. We love each other very much."

"I appreciate your telling me about this. If there's anything I can do to help you, let me know."

Anne looked at her cup of hot chocolate. I could see the tears in her eyes.

"Sorry, I just get kind of emotional lately."

"Is that what the argument up in the choir loft was about?"

"No, that person doesn't even know I'm pregnant. But when they find out, it'll be a lot worse than what you heard. It's complicated."

"Does anyone at the convent know?"

"No, nobody. But they will soon. I can't hide it much longer."

"What do you think they'll do when they find out?"

"I'll have to leave as soon as I tell them—or as soon as they find out. I'm making plans right now. In fact, I was kind of wondering if you could come and play a few Sunday services when I leave, in case I can't find anyone to take over soon enough."

Oh, God, that was the last thing I wanted to do, especially after I'd told David that I was done with churches, nuns, and priests. But I couldn't say no.

"I'll be glad to help out," I said, meaning the opposite. "Just as long as you or someone can find a substitute fast. The organ isn't my thing. I can't play it nearly as well as you can. If I could play the piano instead, it wouldn't be an issue, but the organ is difficult for me."

"You'll do great. You know how simple church music is."

"Okay. Just let me know when I'll be starting so I have time to prepare."

"I can make it through Christmas, I hope. I wouldn't wish Christmas Masses on anyone. Maybe sometime in January. It'll be easy then. Just regular hymns."

We finished our drinks, and I headed home with plans to come and play the Steinway again the following week. I wasn't excited to share this latest development with David. At least it didn't involve a murder—just playing for a few Masses. We'd have a few laughs about my speech from the previous evening. It didn't take long for me to go back on every single one of the promises I had made.

CHAPTER 2

Early December, 1970

Sister Anne played the last notes of Widor's "Toccata," and the sound echoed in the cavernous church for ten seconds before it faded into complete silence.

She then began a simple Bach piece, but heard footsteps ascending the narrow staircase to the choir loft.

"Beautiful!" the visitor said.

"Thank you," Sister Anne replied. "I'm glad to stop for a few minutes. I'm tired of practicing."

"I have something for you. I don't want to fight anymore. I'm really sorry about last time and the things I said." The visitor walked to the front pew in the choir loft, holding a large thermos with a cowboy and horse from an old 50's TV program.

"Where did you get that?" Sister Anne stared at the thermos, wondering where it had come from.

"Don't even ask. It's hot chocolate, your favorite, and it's all for you. I don't like it."

"More for me." Sister Anne laughed as she slid off the bench and sat in the old wooden pew.

"I put it in this to keep it warm."

The huge church was freezing. The temperature outside hovered in the thirties, and she guessed the choir loft wasn't much higher than fifty degrees. The parish never turned the heat on in the church unless there was going to be a Mass. Sister Anne guessed there would be more people visiting the church if it were warmer, but she wouldn't get as much practice time.

"Here, have some before it gets cold."

The cup of steaming hot chocolate looked awfully good as it was held out to her.

"It's nice of you to bring me this." Sister Anne took a sip, not wanting to burn her tongue, but it was already cool enough to drink.

"I know how you like it. Whole milk, just enough sugar, not too hot."

"Yum." She warmed her hands on the odd-looking cup. She took three big gulps of the chocolate, and her hands and her insides got toasty. She sat back in the hard pew. "Are you sure you don't want any?"

"No. It's all for you. When you're done, could you play that Bach piece you've been working on? I love it. And then maybe we can talk—about last time."

"Okay, but I'm going to finish this first." She took another drink of the hot chocolate, poured the last bit from the thermos into the cup, finished that, then jumped up and sat back down on the organ bench, thumbing through the music at her side. She began to play again.

The visitor listened appreciatively, watching her carefully.

Suddenly Sister Anne clutched her stomach and moaned. She stopped playing and grabbed the wooden sides of the organ.

"What's wrong?" The visitor stood, looking concerned.

"I don't know. I have to stop. I feel terrible. My stomach."

She half-climbed, half-stumbled off the bench, and sat on the wooden pew. The blood drained from her face as she slumped over on the seat, her eyes closing.

The visitor asked kindly, "Can I do anything?"

Sister Anne fell over completely on the pew, her right arm positioned beneath her at an odd angle, her mouth open.

There was no answer. The visitor calmly checked Sister Anne's pulse, waited a few seconds longer, checked again, then picked up the cup, wiped the hot chocolate drips from the pew, and rubbed the back of the pew with a napkin. The visitor put on rubber gloves, removed Sister Anne's watch, reset it, then hit it repeatedly on the pew until it broke. The watch was replaced on Sister Anne's arm.

The visitor peered over the low wall at the edge of the loft, took one last look around the empty church, gathered the thermos, cup, and napkins, then walked down the steps, turned off the lights, and exited through the choir door, making sure to close it carefully.

★ ★ ★

"Have you seen Sister Anne?" asked Sister Therese. The five nuns were seated at the dining room table for dinner, and there was one empty place.

Sister Claire, the tall, thin science teacher, shook her head. "Maybe she had band practice?"

"I don't think so," Sister Gloria said. "The band room was closed when I left school."

Sister Joan, who worked in the church office, commented, "I've only seen her at dinner this week."

Sister Frances got up to start clearing the dinner plates from the table but said nothing.

The subject of the fair was brought up, and the conversation went in another direction.

As they were clearing the dishes after dessert, Sister Therese, the superior, said, "If any of you see Sister Anne, tell her to knock on my door when she gets back. She really needs to let us know when she won't be here for dinner." All the sisters nodded in agreement, although it wasn't that unusual for someone to miss dinner. The convent sisters taught in the grade school and high school, and on any given night there were meetings, practices, student council, parent meetings, lessons for students who needed extra tutoring. But it *was* unusual for a nun not to let someone know what was happening and where they were, especially if she was going to miss dinner.

At ten-thirty, Sister Gloria knocked on Sister Therese's door. Sister Therese got up from her desk. Her veil was off and she wore a thin white bathrobe.

She opened the door a crack. "Yes?"

"I wanted to let you know that Sister Anne isn't back yet. It doesn't look like she's been in her room at all."

Sister Therese grabbed her veil, put it on her head, and walked out the door and up the stairs to Sister Anne's room, with Sister Gloria at her side.

"I didn't want to say much at dinner, but this really makes me angry," Sister Therese said. "She should at least have the decency to call and let us know where she is."

Sister Gloria frowned. "She goes out a lot, but I don't think she's ever been out this late. Maybe something's wrong."

Sister Therese didn't move. Sister Gloria said quietly, "Do you think we should do something?"

"Do what?" Sister Therese sounded upset.

"Well, maybe we should call the police."

"The police? They have more important things to do than find someone who's out too late." Sister Therese stood a moment at Sister Anne's door. "I'm going to write a note asking her to wake me up when she gets home. She has a key."

She walked into Sister Anne's room, pulled open a drawer, and found paper and a pen.

★ ★ ★

Sister Therese woke up to the sound of her alarm clock at six thirty. She sat up in bed, knowing she had to be in school by eight fifteen for homeroom. As she walked to the bathroom and was brushing her teeth, she suddenly remembered that no one had woken her during the night. She walked down the long corridor to Sister Anne's room, her morning meditation already ruined.

The door stood wide open. The note remained on the desk. Perhaps Sister Anne hadn't noticed it? The bed was neatly made. She could have returned home late and missed it, then gotten up early and made her bed, but that seemed unlikely.

All this bother for nothing. Sister Therese strode loudly down the corridor, not even bothering to silence her heavy shoes. She got to the chapel for morning prayers at seven thirty. Sister Anne wasn't there. After prayers, they all sat down for breakfast.

Sister Therese clenched her teeth, "Has anyone seen Sister Anne?"

All the nuns looked down. No one said a word.

"Okay, this is too much. Sister Gloria, could you check the school after breakfast? Sister Joan, could you check the church? Sister Claire, see me after breakfast! Thank you all. And let me know right away if you find out anything. I know you all need to be in school, but I need to find her."

All the nuns wandered out except for Sister Claire. She was in her twenties, about the same age as Sister Anne, but they weren't friends.

Sister Therese said, "Sister Anne has some friends outside of school. At least, she seems to spend a lot of time with them. Do you know who they are?"

"Yes, Sister. I know she has one friend named Kristen. That girl who comes and plays the piano in the sitting room. I think they were in the convent together."

"Do you have a phone number for her?"

"No, I have no idea. And she has one other friend. Stacy Richards. I know she has three kids in school, one in high school, so we'd have her number on file. I think Sister Anne spends a lot of time at her place, but there's no way she'd spend the night without telling someone."

"Can you get the number?"

"Sure. I'll be back in a few minutes."

Sister Joan came in the door to the small kitchen, out of breath. "I checked the church. There was no one there. I glanced up at the choir loft, but it was dark and the door was closed."

Sister Therese waited for Sister Claire, and soon she returned with a number for Stacy Richards.

Sister Therese reminded herself to count to ten before dialing the number. This wasn't Mrs. Richards' fault; it was Sister Anne's responsibility.

"Hello, Mrs. Richards?"

"Yes?"

"This is Sister Therese, the principal at Holy Trinity."

"Oh, God, is this about one of my kids?"

"Oh, no, don't worry. I was wondering if you had seen Sister Anne recently."

"Recently? I guess I saw her about a month ago, but we didn't even talk then."

"Oh." Sister Therese was surprised. "I thought she spent a lot of time over at your house."

"My place? No, she's only been here once, a few months ago, right after school started. I wanted Jake to take piano lessons, but it didn't fit with our schedules."

"Oh, okay. Sorry to bother you. You have a nice day. Thank you."

Sister Therese placed the black phone back in its cradle. Then she opened the desk drawer, pulled out the Yellow Pages and turned to page one for the Kirkwood Police number. She picked up the receiver again.

CHAPTER 3

Early December 1970

David called me from work around four thirty on Wednesday, which was unusual.

"Hi, honey. I need to ask you a question. What's the name of that sister you've been seeing every Thursday?"

"Sister Anne. Anne Holtmeyer. Why?"

"Just wondering. I'm going to be home a little early tonight. How about if I pick up some dinner?"

"That sounds wonderful. What's the occasion?"

"No occasion. Because I love you. I'll see you in about an hour. Bye."

David walked in the door a little later and greeted the two kitties, who were very excited to see him. They both loved David and jumped up on his lap whenever they had the chance.

"What did you get for me?" I peered into the takeout bag.

"I played it safe and got lasagna."

"That's always a good bet. Thanks for getting it. I've been studying. Just one more exam and I'm done. Except for the prac-tice teaching. I can't believe it. I'm so excited."

David was unusually quiet during the meal. We ate and had a glass of wine, but I realized I had done most of the talking, which was unusual. He usually had a lot to say about his day, sharing various humorous stories, articles from the newspaper, and his political opinions.

"Are you okay?" I finally asked.

"No, I'm not. I couldn't tell you this over the phone, but come over to the couch with me. I have something to tell you."

I had a terrible feeling it was bad news. But what?

"That Sister Anne you've been seeing lately at St. Boniface Parish? She was murdered last night. They found her body in the choir loft this morning, and we were called to investigate."

I couldn't say a word; I started crying. David put his arms around me and held me tightly.

"I can't believe this is happening—again," I stuttered between sobs. "She was so wonderful, and I was just getting to know her."

I couldn't stop crying. David got up to fetch a box of tissues. Both cats jumped onto me, curious about why I was crying. Alex licked my hand and JC crawled onto my lap. I wished I could explain to them.

"Do you want something to drink?"

"No. I need to sit here for a while."

David went into the other room to let me be alone, but came in every so often to check on me.

"Do you want to talk?" he finally asked.

"I guess. There's a lot of things you'll need to know."

"What do you mean?"

"I can't tell you tonight, but tomorrow morning, we need to have a talk. Like it or not, I'm in the middle of this murder, like all the rest. Oh, I feel so sorry for her. I can't believe it."

He held me again—for a long time—until all my tears were gone and I simply couldn't cry anymore.

The next morning I got up late, and David was waiting for me at the breakfast table.

"Did you sleep at all?"

"Not much. I suppose I did, a little."

"You were awfully restless. You tossed and turned all night."

"I should have slept in the other bedroom. I'm sorry; I didn't realize I would keep you awake."

"I'm fine. You didn't keep me awake—well, a little, but it's okay. I have to go in to work pretty soon. Do you want to tell me those things now?"

"They're about Sister Anne. Do you need to know today? Are you starting the investigation right away?"

"No, we can wait till this evening. I have a lot at work to finish up before I start working on this. And you have your exam today."

"Yeah. I hope I can get through it."

"You will. Clear everything else from your mind for now. There will be plenty of time later to think about it."

"You're right. I'll try my best."

"Good luck. I love you."

★ ★ ★

It wasn't easy, but I tried to follow David's suggestion. I pushed the murder out of my mind and kept telling myself I would think about it later. I focused on the questions in the exam. Once I finished, I would complete my English degree at Washington University. At that moment, I had only the desire to do well and finish it. I concentrated hard. The two hours passed quickly, and I did better than I'd anticipated. I submitted my paper and left the room.

By the time I got to my car, the reality of the murder hit me. I started crying as I sat in my car, before I even started the engine. I didn't care who walked by or who saw me. Someone mouthed, "Are you okay?" through the window, and I managed a weak smile and said yes, then decided to drive home quickly.

I went to bed, attempting to get some much-needed sleep, but Alex and JC meowed at the bedroom door, keeping me awake.

Finally, David got home. I walked out to see him. I'm sure I looked terrible with my bloodshot eyes and messy hair, but he hugged me and asked if I was okay.

I nodded.

He said, "Let's sit down on the couch and you can tell me these things you needed to tell me."

We sat close to each other and he held my hand.

"You know, I've been playing music with Sister Anne all month, and we've gotten to know each other quite well. Each time I went, I practiced for at least an hour on their beautiful piano, and then we headed to a nearby drugstore for a drink."

"How did they get such an expensive piano?"

"An old lady had it in her home, and when she couldn't play any longer, having no family, she gave it to the sisters."

"That was a nice gift. Those things are expensive, aren't they?"

"Very expensive. I hope I can get one someday, but that doesn't seem very likely. Anyway, the first day I went there and returned the music to Anne, I heard her arguing with someone in the choir loft. She yelled at them to get out of there, and someone threw something, maybe a book. The person left, came down the steps, and went outside. I didn't turn around to see who it was. It wasn't any of my business. I waited until Anne started playing, and I went upstairs. I asked her about it, but she said she was okay."

"I wish you had seen who it was. Was it a man or a woman?"

"I don't know. They never said anything and like I said, I didn't see them. The first time I visited Anne, she told me she was unhappy, that she didn't have any friends, and that it was hard to make friends in a small mission. But then we talked about music and the piano."

"I'll need to find out who she had that argument with, and what it was about."

"I have lots more to tell you."

"Okay, go on."

"Eventually she told me something else that you need to know. She was about ready to leave the order. Probably right after Christmas, if she could wait that long. She was pregnant, and she knew people would find out about it very soon."

"What? Oh, there are so many people who could have been angry about that. Did she tell you who the father is?"

"No, she wouldn't tell me that, but she said she loved him and that he wasn't free to be with her yet, but that soon he was going to marry her, and they'd be a family together."

"What was she going to do in the meantime?"

"Stay with her parents."

"Did she really think the man was going to follow through and help her?"

"She seemed to think so. She said they loved each other, and she trusted him."

David frowned. "If she said he wasn't free to be with her yet, he was probably married, or going through a divorce. So it could have been the father who killed her, or his wife if he was married, or the superior of the convent when she found out about the pregnancy, or another jealous sister, or anybody. There are a lot of possible motives. I'm really glad you have some insight into this whole situation. This gives me a lot to work with. Too much, actually."

"That's the first time you've ever thanked me for interfering in an investigation."

"You haven't interfered in anything. It wasn't an investigation until today, and you found all this out as a friend. That's completely different."

"Oh, and there's something else. Remember that Anne asked me to play for her when she left? I told you about that and we laughed about it? I guess I should offer to play for them, at least for a while, until they find someone. I'll tell them Anne asked me."

"Are you sure you can handle it?"

"You mean musically or emotionally?"

"Well, both, I guess."

"I can do it musically, because I know how to play the organ. Not as well as the piano, but I know the liturgy very well."

"What's the liturgy?"

"What songs are supposed to be sung for each part of the Mass and which songs go with the readings of the day. There's a lot to know. As for emotionally, I don't know how I'll feel being up there, where she was murdered. I'll have to see when I go up there—if they even want me. Maybe they'll find someone else. That would be the best thing."

"I think so. I hope so, for your sake."

CHAPTER 4

I called St. Boniface the next day and asked to talk to the pastor. The receptionist told me he was busy, but when I explained why I was calling, she assured me he would call back as soon as possible. After all, they were without a music director and organist, and would need someone for the next weekend, at the very least.

Rather than a call from the pastor, I received a call from Sister Therese, the superior of the convent.

"Kristen?"

"Yes."

"This is Sister Therese, from St. Boniface Convent. I know you were a friend of Sister Anne's, and I wondered if you'd like to come over here and go through some of her piano music. We don't know what to do with it, and I'm sure you would know better than anyone else the best place for it."

"I appreciate that, Sister. I'm sure Sister Anne would want it to go to people who could use it, maybe to a college or a teacher."

"Someone will be here whenever you'd like to stop by. Just let us know when you plan to come."

"I'll try to come as soon as I can. All my classes are over now, so I can come any time."

* * *

I knocked on the convent door, and Sister Therese answered it.

"Thank you for coming. Come in."

We walked into the large room with the piano. I was familiar with it, and I knew where all the music was kept.

"If you could go through some of this music, we'd appreciate it. I'm sure someone could use it."

"I'll do my best, Sister."

"We're all so shocked at what happened. I can't believe Sister Anne was murdered. And the police are questioning all of us here at the convent. I'm sure it was the father of her child who killed her. I guess you know all about that by now. Everyone does."

"Yes, Sister Anne told me about it a few weeks ago when we were talking. She said no one knew that she was pregnant."

"No one knew, but we would have found out soon enough. She would have had to leave, that's for sure."

"She asked me if I would play over at the church for her after she left."

"She did?"

"Yes, but I told her I hoped the parish would find someone else to play."

"Well, I don't have anything to do with that. You should talk to the pastor, Father John."

"I have an appointment with Father Michael later today. He's the assistant pastor?"

"Yes. I think Sister Anne worked more with him than with the pastor."

I sat down on an old, brocaded chair and started to go through Anne's music. She had quite a selection of pieces, from Bach to Chopin to Debussy. There wasn't much contemporary music, but a lot of the classics, like Beethoven, Handel, and Haydn. I spent over an hour going through her collection.

I wasn't sure what could be done with most of it. I would reach out to the music professors at the university to see if they could use any of the music, but beyond that, I couldn't imagine who else might want any of it. I needed to ask if her parents or family would like some of the music. Maybe someone else in her family played.

I had seen a fast-food place a few blocks from the convent, so I drove there for lunch. I didn't want to ask anyone at the convent for food and no one came in to ask me if I wanted anything. My appointment with Father Michael was at 2 p.m.

I walked across the street and into the church offices. There was a nun at the front desk; I guessed she was the secretary. She introduced herself as Sister Joan. I told her I had an appointment with Father Michael. She gave me a strange look, as if I didn't belong there, but got up and led me down the hall to his office.

Sister Joan knocked on the first office door.

"Come in, come in," boomed a friendly voice. I walked in the office and stared at Father Michael. He was probably the most handsome man I had ever seen. I felt like a traitor to David, but then I looked at Father Michael again. No, sorry, he *was* the most handsome. He should have been on a movie set. Black wavy hair, deep blue eyes. A perfect smile with white teeth, a smile that could light up a room. Dimples, a flawless complexion, a little tanned—even in winter. He reached out and clasped my hand.

"Sit down. How can I help you?"

"I'm Kristen, a friend of Sister Anne's."

His face changed immediately to complete sadness. I kept talking.

"I knew Sister Anne when I was in the convent. She was a few years ahead of me. I brought her some music about a month ago and we caught up since I hadn't seen her for years. Anyway, I played the beautiful piano over in the convent, and we started talking, and Sister Anne told me a few weeks ago that she might be leaving here soon. She asked if I could substitute for her when she did leave. Of course, no one ever expected this to happen, but I want to say I'm available as an organist in case you need someone to take over for a few weeks and help with the liturgy."

Father Michael looked so upset that I wanted to reach out and grab his hand again and tell him that everything would be all right.

He finally looked up at me. I could see tears in his eyes.

"I can't believe she was killed right here in the church. It's such a shock to all of us. I don't think we've even thought about what's going to happen in the next few weeks, but you're absolutely right. We need to. Your offer is generous, and yes, we do need someone to take over for the month of December. I assume you're fully qualified to take over the playing and know the liturgy?"

"I just graduated from Washington University with my degree in English, and I also have a minor in music. I play the piano and organ and I'm very familiar with the liturgy from the convent, although I've never been a director of music or anything like that. I'm sure I can take over for a few weeks until you find someone who's more qualified."

"I have no idea what she had planned as far as music and the liturgy. We were going to have a meeting a few days ago. You'll have to talk with some members of her choir. They meet on Thursday night, tomorrow night, and you can ask them what they've been working on. Some of them might know what she was planning to play for the Christmas Masses, although I'm not even sure of that. I really appreciate your offer, though. You and I can coordinate everything together, maybe on Friday if you have the time. Do you have another job?"

"No. I just graduated, so all my classes are finished and I'm waiting for my final grades. I have some free time."

"Well, that's perfect. Why don't we meet back here on Friday afternoon? If you could come to choir practice tomorrow evening, you'll get a much better idea of what the Christmas season will be like. I'll give you a key to the church and also to Sister Anne's office so you can check that out too. I'll show you where it is."

We walked down the long corridor from the office building to the church. Sister Anne's office was in one of the side buildings next to the church.

Father Michael said, "I'll leave you here to look through some of her music and papers. You'll probably get a clue of what she had planned in the next few weeks. Make sure to lock up when you leave. Thanks. And stop by Father John's office on the way out to introduce yourself so we can get the paperwork done. Thank you so much for your offer to do this."

"Okay, I'm glad I can help out. I'll be here on Friday."

"Good."

CHAPTER 5

I opened the old wooden door and looked inside the cramped room. Sister Anne's office had a small desk, a telephone, papers everywhere, and shelves of hymnals and sheet music for the church congregation and choirs. There was a worn grey couch, and the white walls needed paint. It was obvious the music office wasn't very important and had been used for lots of other things before it became a music office. I saw some old bells from church and a rusted iron bed frame leaning against the back wall. It looked like the dumping ground for unused parish items. An aching sadness filled my chest—she would never be coming back. And my anger grew for the person who had killed her.

I couldn't go through her music. I just sat at the desk for a while. A large window opened to an atrium filled with trees, and the view was beautiful, even in winter. I imagined that in the spring there would be leaves, flowers, and birds on the branches of the trees. I could see what appeared to be a large hall across the atrium, but at least some nature was outside the window instead of brick walls. I closed the window drapes tightly to see how private the office was. In here, she could be very alone, or with someone else. She could have gotten pregnant right here. It could have been with anyone. All the man had to do was come from the back of the church, walk down the corridor, and knock on her office door.

I locked the office and walked down the corridor into the church. Even though the sun was shining outside, the church was a tomb, gloomy and depressing. The door to the choir loft stood open, so I climbed the stairs. There was a large stained-glass window halfway up the steps. It was hidden from anyone but the person who walked up the enclosed stairs, and the light shone only on the stairs. What a waste of a window—and poor planning.

The steps took a sharp right turn, and I climbed to the door of the loft. The dim ceiling lights illuminated the dark wooden pews on each side of the organ. It was a large pipe organ, with silver pipes covering the entire back wall, but I had no desire to turn it on yet. Police tape still covered the organ bench and part of the organ. I didn't dare disturb it.

What a contrast to my last visit here. We'd laughed and had such a wonderful time listening to each other play, even though most of the time we ended up at the convent to play the piano.

She had been killed right here just a few days ago. I didn't know any of the details. I wasn't sure I even wanted to know. I shivered, turned around, and escaped down the stairs.

I walked back to the office and told Sister Joan that I needed to see Father John about some paperwork. She called his office and told him I'd be coming by, and then she led me down the corridor to another office door and left me.

I knocked on the door. He called out, "Come in."

Father John was an older priest, probably in his late fifties; I couldn't tell. He looked like one of my professors at school, clean-shaven and neat. His black hair was cut mid-length, not too short. He wasn't bad looking for his age. He wore his Roman collar and a black shirt with long sleeves. He didn't seem very friendly, but he handed me a packet of papers to fill out so I could work for the parish.

"Just bring these back the next time you come. I hear you're going to take over for Sister Anne for a while."

"Yes, but I hope you can find someone very soon. I'm helping out in the meantime."

"Well, we appreciate it. It was such a terrible thing that happened. I still can't believe it. And right here in the church. Did you know her well?"

"No, we had just gotten to know each other in the last month, actually. She was such a good person."

"Yes, she appeared to be. We don't interact with the sisters very often, except during the liturgy and with the sister who works in the front office. Otherwise, we don't see much of them. They're so busy with their school duties, and we have our parish responsibilities."

He didn't seem to have much emotion about Anne's death, but he didn't seem to know her very well.

"Thank you for offering to play. We're putting a notice in the archdiocese newsletter for a new organist and choir director. It goes out to all the parishes this Sunday, so hopefully it won't be too long before we can find someone."

I walked out the large front door of the church, eager to be in the sun. It felt cold, but good.

★ ★ ★

David and I went to Steak and Shake that evening for dinner. He was tired and so was I.

"Did you go to the church today?" he asked.

"Yeah, but it was pretty uneventful. I met the two priests, but that was all."

"I'll be interviewing them in the next few days. I need to interview all the priests and nuns in the parish. They're the first suspects in the investigation, unfortunately. I wish we had a clue who the father of Anne's baby was."

"Well, I don't think you'll find out much from the priests. They didn't seem to have much interaction with the nuns, except for talking about the liturgy."

"Oh, yeah, that stuff that goes in the Mass and everything—the songs and pieces you play."

"Yeah, that stuff. But other than that, they were sad, but not terribly upset. Father Michael was more upset about her death than Father John, but that might be their personalities and their ways of expressing themselves."

"Which one is which?"

"Father Michael is the younger priest who worked with her most on the liturgy. Father John is the pastor; he's older and didn't seem to know her very well. She had started in September."

"Well, I'll be talking with them tomorrow."

CHAPTER 6

David drove up to the church and parked his car. As he walked past the rectory where the priests lived, he noticed two cars in the garage. Both appeared to be a few years old. The nuns, all six of them, had only one used car, while each priest received a new car every few years. David wondered if the priests took a vow of poverty like the nuns did. He would have to ask Kristen about it that evening.

He couldn't believe he was here, interviewing people about another convent murder—one that Kristen was involved in again. Not directly, but she'd known the victim and had become friends with her. It was as if she couldn't escape her past, no matter how hard she tried. He felt so sorry for her. He wanted to solve this murder quickly and hoped it didn't implicate the sisters in the convent itself. It seemed likely that the murderer was the father of the child who couldn't face his obligation to Sister Anne and the baby. Finding that person was the most important part of the investigation—and would be the most difficult. He walked to the church office, a brick building that was showing its age.

A nun was sitting at the front desk. He identified himself and asked to speak to Father Michael. Sister Joan walked down the corridor with him, smiling and obsequious. She stayed by his side until Father Michael called for him to come in.

The priest rose from his chair and shook hands with David. He invited him to sit down across from the large desk. David didn't want to spend too much time on these interviews. He thought they might be a waste of time, but he had to be careful. The truth was almost always unexpected. He told the priest the conversation would be recorded.

"Father, how well did you know the deceased, Sister Anne?"

Father Michael shook his head. "Such a shame. A tragedy. Whatever I can do to help. I knew her slightly. We would meet on Thursday afternoons to discuss the music that would be played and sung the following Sunday. They were very short meetings. She knew what she was doing—picking music that went with the readings of the day or whatever feast day it was. She was very good at that. I didn't have to worry about her selections at all. We never really talked much. And never about anything personal."

"Where were you the afternoon that Sister Anne was murdered? It was last Wednesday afternoon."

"Of course. That was my day off. In the afternoon, I had lunch with my friend Father Gregory. He's the pastor at St. Timothy's in Clayton and was my teacher in the seminary."

"When did you get back from lunch?"

"I got back here around four o'clock. I saw Sister Joan when I got back and then went to my room in the rectory."

"Can you think of anyone who would have wanted to harm Sister Anne? You do know she was pregnant."

He shook his head again sadly. "Yes, I do. Sister Joan told me last week after the funeral. Such a shame. No, I don't know anyone. I suppose you should be looking for the father of the child. Maybe he was a married man and couldn't face the consequences of his actions. I can't imagine anyone killing her. She'd only been here for a few months. She probably didn't even know that many people."

"Do you have any idea who the father might be?"

"Absolutely not. Like I said, I met her once a week to discuss the liturgy, and I occasionally heard her practicing if I was in the church, but I didn't really know her. I don't know who her friends were. The sisters would be better able to answer that question."

"Thank you, Father. Can we have the phone number of Father Gregory? To confirm where you were."

"Of course." He wrote it down and handed it to David. "Do you want to see Father John? I'll take you to his office."

David followed Father Michael down the passageway to another office. The door was open.

"Father John, this is Detective Kelly."

"Oh, yes." Father John got up and shook hands with David. "Please sit down."

"I need to ask you a few questions about Sister Anne," David said.

He set up the tape recorder and began the interview.

"How well did you know Sister Anne?"

The priest looked up at the ceiling for a few minutes. "I saw her every so often in the church, practicing. Well, I heard her, really. I haven't been up in the choir loft in months. Father Michael took care of the liturgy."

"Did you know of anyone who disliked her?"

"No, I wouldn't know anything about that. She's only been here a short time, since September, when the school year began. Father Michael and I are very busy with the parish, and we don't really get to know any of the sisters. Except for Sister Joan, of course, who works with us in the office."

"You did know Sister Anne was pregnant at the time of her death?"

"Yes, yes, I heard about that last week after her death. What a scandal that would have been. Of course, she would have had the baby, but she wouldn't have been able to stay in the convent any longer."

"Father, where were you last Wednesday afternoon?"

"I knew you'd ask that question, so I already checked my calendar. I was at Forest Hills Nursing Home, administering the sacraments to the residents there."

"Were you there the whole afternoon?"

"I was there from about one thirty to three thirty. You can check with Cecelia Carver. She's the coordinator there. There was a gentleman who needed the last rites that afternoon. He passed away at about three fifteen. I came back after that."

"And what did you do when you returned to the church?"

"I went to my room in the rectory for a few minutes, then I had a meeting at four with a parishioner for counseling."

"I'm sorry, Father, but I'll need the name of that parishioner."

"Of course. I'll give it to you on the way out."

"Thank you, Father."

David had some time to interview a nun at the parish, so he headed over to the convent. He rang the bell, and when Sister Frances answered, he introduced himself. When she got flustered and asked who he wanted to talk to, he asked if the superior of the convent was home.

Sister Frances was anxious to leave the room and fetch her.

Sister Therese was clearly uncomfortable talking to David. He didn't know if it was because he was from the police department or if she was worried about her answers, but she kept wringing her hands and sweating.

"Sister, why didn't you check the church earlier if you knew Sister Anne practiced there in the afternoon?"

"She didn't practice every afternoon. Just a few times a week. Other times she was visiting her friend, staying at school, or she might have been in her office. She could have been in any number of places. We had no idea that something was wrong until later that evening, and then the next morning. We did check the church and the school that evening."

David said, "Sister Anne's watch had been deliberately broken by some object, and it stopped at two thirty-seven on Wednesday afternoon. Where were you at that time, Sister?"

"I was still at school. In fact, I think you'll find that most of us were. Sister Anne's last class is earlier, though. The final bell doesn't even ring until two forty-five."

"Were you teaching or in your office?"

"I don't have a seventh-period class, but I was in my office at school. My secretary and everyone in the office can verify that."

"How did you get along with Sister Anne?"

David noticed tears welling up in her eyes. He didn't think he could cry on command like that. *Now, be charitable. Maybe she really does feel bad.*

"She was a wonderful addition to our little family here. Everyone loved her."

She dabbed her eyes with a tissue that David provided from the box next to him.

"Did you know that Sister Anne was pregnant at the time of her death?"

"Oh, those were just terrible rumors, sir. I, for one, don't believe them at all."

"Well, Sister, it's true. She was a few months pregnant."

"I wasn't aware of *that*. I'm sure nobody else was either."

"If you had known, Sister, what would you have done, as the superior of the convent?"

Sister Therese blushed and stammered, "Well, I don't know. She would have had the child somewhere else. She couldn't have stayed here. We would have found out who the father was and made sure he took responsibility for the child."

"She wouldn't have been able to stay in the order, would she?"

"Oh, no. She would have had to leave."

"Is that what happens in those situations?"

Sister Therese looked horrified. "Our order has never had a situation like that. This would have been the first. These things don't happen in our order."

"Okay. Thank you for your time. We'll be talking to you again soon." David glanced at the list of nuns in his notebook. "Could you ask Sister Gloria to come in?"

Sister Gloria was thin and wiry with boundless energy, eager to answer questions.

She had been teaching English at the time of the murder.

"How did you feel about Sister Anne?"

Sister Gloria praised her enthusiastically. "She was an incredible musician. I adored listening to her play."

"You would go up in the choir loft with her?" David asked.

"No, I would go into the church and listen some afternoons. She always practiced around the same time, after school and before dinner. I love the organ, and she was a true musician. It was a joy to hear her play."

"Did she practice every day?"

"No, she was so busy. But every so often I would hear her when I was walking home after school, and I'd slip in to listen. Not very often. Neither one of us had much time."

"How well did you really know her?"

"She was very shy. Musicians are like that. I think she released her emotions when she played. She wasn't much for talking. I guess I really didn't know her that well."

"You knew she was pregnant?"

"She never told me directly, but she told Sister Claire first, and the news spread very quickly, as you can imagine. Nobody knew what was going to happen to her. She didn't know either.

We figured she had a few more months before she had to leave. You know, before it became obvious."

CHAPTER 7

David interviewed only the two sisters that first day.

I had time to prepare fresh salmon and broccoli that evening. We sat down and David talked a little about the investigation, as much as he could without revealing very much.

"I never told you about her watch. It was shattered."

"Did it break when she fell?"

"I'm sorry. I thought I told you. No, it had been deliberately broken. That's how we know the time of the murder."

We talked a little longer, but he didn't have much more to say about the case.

I woke up that night wondering how he was going to solve this murder. The murderer had to be the father, but how would he ever find out who the father was? The man wasn't going to announce it. And David couldn't interview every man in the city of Kirkwood.

I turned on the little night-light on my side of the bed and glanced at my watch. One fifteen. I had to get some sleep. I didn't want to wake David since he was a very light sleeper. The clock on the wall read one twenty-five. My watch was slow. I pulled out the little button to reset it and turned off the night-light.

Then I pictured the murder scene. Sister Anne, dead, lying on the pew in the choir loft. What if the man or woman took her watch, reset it, then smashed it and put it back on her arm? That way, the murderer would have a perfect alibi. Would they set it ahead? They might. But they'd probably set it back when they already had an alibi, like teaching the last period of school or being somewhere else. Well, it *was* possible. I had to remember to tell David in the morning. Except I was sure he had already thought of that.

I was awakened by the persistent meows of JC, who was a lot louder than Alex. Luckily, David was already out of bed. I got dressed quickly and walked out in the kitchen to get breakfast. I stood looking at the Rice Chex, the Raisin Bran, and the oatmeal for a long time.

"Why are you just standing there?" David finally asked.

"Oh, I'm thinking about something else," I said as I grabbed the oatmeal.

I sat down with the oatmeal and hot chocolate and told him about the watch.

"Do you think it would be possible to change the watch to make it fit an alibi, so whoever it was would be somewhere else at the time she was murdered, and you would just assume that was the time of death?"

David sat quietly. "I think you could be right. We might have to have to expand the time of the murder to that whole afternoon. That might wipe out a lot of alibis if it's true. Let's just assume it is."

David went to the convent for the next set of interviews, while I went to the church to practice all the music I needed to play for Christmas.

CHAPTER 8

The next afternoon, David's first interview was with Sister Claire. She was around twenty-five years old and beautiful. Her blond hair stuck out from under her veil, but her face was perfect, with naturally red lips.

"What were you doing last Wednesday when Sister Anne was killed?"

"You don't think that I killed her!" She sounded almost angry that David would ask the question.

"Sister, I have to ask everyone that question. It doesn't mean I think you murdered Sister Anne."

"Well"—she sounded a little calmer. "I was finishing up at school in the lab until after three. I don't teach that last period, but I think I was still in the lab."

"Is there anyone who might have seen you?"

"No, everyone else was still teaching. And all my students were gone."

"How did you get along with Sister Anne?"

"She was okay. Quiet. She had only been here a few months. I didn't know her very well."

"Did Sister Anne spend a lot of time away from the convent?"

"Well, she taught during the day, and she 'practiced' every afternoon." The word 'practice' was a sneer.

"You don't think she was really practicing?"

"I don't know, I guess. There were lots of times when we thought she was practicing, but the choir loft was dark and locked, so she was going somewhere else—at least, part of the time. She said she visited her friend Stacy Richards, but I have no idea if that's where she was. And she had time to get pregnant, didn't she?"

"You knew she was pregnant at the time of her death?"

Sister Claire hesitated, then said very quietly, "Of course. Everyone did. She had morning sickness and Sister Therese questioned her, and she admitted she was pregnant, but she wouldn't say who the father was."

"What did you think about that? About her being pregnant?"

"Well, she wasn't anything to look at. I can't imagine her finding someone so quickly."

David cringed at her uncharitable, sexist comment, but said nothing. It was best to let her keep talking.

"I mean, it was wrong and everything. It was a terrible sin, and she would have had to leave. And I don't know what *he* was going to do."

"Do you know who the father was?"

"Oh, no, I didn't mean that," Sister Claire shot back immediately. "I have no idea. She wouldn't tell anyone."

"It seems like you didn't see her often."

"Just at meals. And she was pretty shy too. Never said much. I would have liked to have gotten to know her, but nobody really has the time. We're all so busy."

"Did she have any enemies? Anyone who didn't like her?"

"Probably the man who got her pregnant. That's what I think. He would have wanted to get rid of her, especially if he were married. I can't imagine that any of us would have wanted to kill her. We hardly knew her."

David asked for Sister Frances next, who wondered if he could interview her closer to the kitchen so she could keep an eye on the meal for the evening. She led him down a dark corridor farther into the house, where a large dining room loomed off to the side. The drapes were dark brown and drawn shut. He guessed they didn't want to waste that precious sunlight on anything in the house. The corridor led to a small sitting room and another one after that. He sat in the small room while Sister Frances left to get him tea. David opened the brown drapes and the light flooded in, exposing the dust on the ancient green carpet. The window overlooked another brick building.

David wondered, not for the first time, why anyone would want to join an order of nuns. Hardly anyone lived in this convent; it didn't seem to be much of a community, and that was the whole point of being a nun, or so he'd thought. They weren't very friendly. The dentist's office was more welcoming and relaxing.

He stopped himself. He always judged things too quickly.

Sister Frances walked tentatively in the door, balancing a tray with two cups of tea.

David started the interview. "Sister, could you tell me where you were last Wednesday afternoon?"

"Well, I was here like I always am, cleaning up and cooking."

"Is there anyone who can vouch for you?"

"No, I was here by myself. But I'm usually here all day by myself. I see the other sisters at breakfast and dinner. And in the evenings, when we watch TV. That's all."

"Did you know that Sister Anne liked hot chocolate?"

"Oh, everybody knew. She made it for breakfast, then had a cup before she went to bed. I didn't mind; I didn't have to make it."

"Did you know her very well?"

"No, but she wasn't around very much. She taught over in the high school, and I guess she practiced a lot at church, had dinner with us, and usually went up to her room right after that. She'd come down to fix her chocolate, but we didn't see her. A few of us would be watching TV, but we could hear her in the kitchen."

"Do you ever go over to the church during the day?"

"No, if I get done with my cleaning and cooking, I try to watch 'Days of our Lives' on weekday afternoons."

"When is it on?"

"At two thirty."

"Were you watching it last Wednesday?"

"I don't remember. I probably was."

"Can you think of anyone who might want to hurt Sister Anne?"

Sister Frances was very quiet. "Sister Anne didn't really seem to be happy here. Not that any of us are."

"What do you mean, Sister?"

"Well, it's not a friendly home. Not like some of the other places I've been. I could see why Sister Anne didn't want to spend much time here. Everybody goes their separate ways."

"Have you ever thought about leaving, Sister?"

"Me? Never. I'm too old. Where would I go? I don't have any family left. I asked Mother Hannah last year if I could be transferred to another mission, but our congregation is very small, and there was no other place for me. I'm only saying I could understand why Sister Anne would like to get out of this house. And no, I don't know anyone who would want to kill her. I thought at first that maybe she killed herself—being pregnant and all that."

"You knew she was pregnant?"

"Of course. We all did. She got very sick with what we thought was the flu, but it was morning sickness. She was out of school for two weeks, at least. I felt bad for her. She couldn't keep anything down. She made a doctor appointment on her own and went. It took her a week to tell any of us."

"Sister Therese told us that she didn't know that Sister Anne was pregnant. Is that true?"

"No, of course not. She was the second or third person to know. We all talked about it a lot—amongst ourselves. Not at the dinner table or anything. Of course she knew."

"Can you think of any reason she would lie to us?"

"Well, Sister Therese was very upset about it. Something like this has never, and I mean never, happened before in our order. And Sister Therese had a lot to lose. Sister Anne had the most to lose, of course. She would have had a child out of wedlock and would have to leave the order. Who knows if the father even knew if she was pregnant? But Sister Therese had her reputation as a superior, and this horrible incident had occurred under her supervision, so to speak. I can understand why she might lie, except that she had to know you'd ask everyone else the same question."

"Did Sister Therese have reason to hurt Sister Anne?"

"Well, I suppose so, but she'd never do that. She's a good person, really."

"Thank you, Sister. I'm sure I'll be talking to you again."

Sister Frances got up slowly, took the empty cups of tea, and walked out of the room.

CHAPTER 9

The next day, David headed back to the parish and interviewed Sister Joan in the parish office.

"I hope this will be quick, Detective. I have an assistant at the parish desk, but she's just started the job."

"I'm sure this won't take too long. You work in the parish office, not the school?"

"Yes, sir, I've worked here for five years."

"And what were you doing last Wednesday afternoon?"

"I was in the back office doing the payroll. Jennifer Haas was answering the phones. We do that every week on Wednesday."

"Is the back office near the main office?"

"It's right next to it."

"So Jennifer could vouch for your whereabouts the whole time?"

"Yes, sir. I finished with the payroll right before she left at three o'clock."

"And what did you do after that?"

"I went back to my desk and worked there until the office closed at five p.m."

"Did anyone see you working there from three to five?"

"No, I don't think so. Father John was away for most of the afternoon, but when he returned, he went to the rectory. Father Michael had gone to his friends for lunch since it was his day off. They were both in and out that afternoon."

"And how did you get along with Sister Anne?"

"She was a young, foolish girl, allowing herself to get pregnant by a man who took advantage of her."

"Do you have any idea who the father might be?"

Sister Joan glanced at her watch. "I have no idea, sir."

"Do you know anyone who might want to take her life?"

"Of course not!" She seemed offended by the question. "I'm sure she was killed by the father of her child. Probably a married man. Oh, I think she was foolish, but I still feel sorry for her. She certainly didn't deserve to die."

"Did you ever see anyone visit her in the church or the music office?"

"No, the priests and I are the only ones here. Well, there's also Emma Huber, the cook at the rectory. But she rarely comes over to the office."

"Did she know Sister Anne?"

"I'm sure she didn't. Maybe she ran into her once or twice, but Emma just cooks the meals and cleans the rectory and then goes home."

"Are there any other people who work at the parish?"

"Yes, the maintenance man, Mr. Miller."

"I'll need to speak with him also. Can you arrange that for tomorrow, Sister Joan?"

"Yes, of course, in the afternoon?"

"Around three would be best."

CHAPTER 10

I drove to St. Boniface that Thursday evening for choir practice, feeling just a little intimidated by the whole situation I had gotten myself into. I walked up the stairs to meet with a group of about twenty-five choir members talking quietly among themselves. They looked at me like I was interrupting their important discussion, which I was.

They were talking about Sister Anne. The choir practice had been canceled last week, so this was the first time they'd had a chance to talk with each other about her murder. Some of them were crying. I felt like an intruder.

I stood in front of the group and introduced myself.

"You're going to have to help me out and tell me what Sister Anne had planned for the Christmas Masses and what you've been practicing. I'll be taking over for a few weeks until the parish can find a replacement. Sister Anne and I were friends from the convent, and she had asked me to help her out in the next few months."

Everyone started speaking all at once. They were more than happy to show me everything they had been learning, and we spent the two hours going through all the music for the next few Sundays, up to and including Christmas. I felt so much better after the practice. I'd need to spend a few long sessions at the organ to familiarize myself with some of the music I would be playing.

When I went in to see Father Michael the next afternoon, I had a typed list of the liturgy for the next few Sundays. We had a good meeting. He seemed very nice. I even wondered if he might be the father of her child. I supposed it was possible. He was around her age, so it was logical, and it would have been easy for them to meet during the day. I should stop thinking about things like that. It meant both of them would have broken their vows, which was pretty unlikely. I couldn't imagine who else she would have met, though, and gotten to know in such a short time. I would let David figure this one out.

CHAPTER 11

On Monday, David interviewed the church employees.

Mr. Miller walked into Father John's office, where David was conducting the interviews.

"What do you do here at the parish?" David began.

Mr. Miller liked to talk and told David more than he ever needed or wanted to know about his duties as gardener, pest controller, handyman, and electrician.

David finally got a word in. "Did you know Sister Anne?"

"No, sir, I don't think I ever met her. I might have seen her coming in and out of church, but I'm not usually working over on that side. I wouldn't be able to point her out individually. I couldn't do that with any of the sisters, though, except for Sister Joan, who works here in the office. It's sad what happened to Sister Anne, though."

"What were you doing last Wednesday afternoon?"

"Well, Wednesday... Let me think. I think that was the day I had to repair the electrical outlets in the hall. I spent most of the afternoon on that."

"Do you have anyone here who could verify that?"

"No, I don't think so. I was in and out of the office and the hall all day, like usual."

"Thank you, Mr. Miller. Would you mind asking Mrs. Huber to come here for her interview?"

"Sure, she's right across the hall. I'll get her."

Mrs. Huber walked into the office. She was a large woman with curly black hair. She wore a brightly colored floral dress and carried a large paper bag.

"Thank you, Mrs. Huber. We need to know where you were last Wednesday afternoon, the day of the murder."

She smiled. "Same as every other day. Dusting and cleaning the rectory, that's where the priests live, and in the afternoon I fixed dinner for the priests. I usually go home after four thirty. I think I fixed fried chicken for them last Wednesday."

"Did you go over to the church at all that day?"

"Yes, sir, I go to Mass every morning, but not the rest of the day. I'm too busy."

"Did you know Sister Anne?"

"No, sir, I didn't know her, but I hear her playing the organ sometimes during the day and on Sundays. She was excellent. Like an angel playing up there."

She hesitated for a second, then held out the paper bag with both hands. "This is silly, but I don't know. I thought I should tell the police."

"What is it?" David opened the bag carefully and took out an old metal thermos with an image of a cowboy and his horse. It looked like it was from the '50 s.

Mrs. Huber started to explain. "I've seen this thermos in the back of the kitchen cupboard for years, but I never used it. It belongs to the priests, I guessed. But I've seen Sister Joan use it in the staff room and sometimes bring a drink to her office. I clean up the staff room sometimes too, and I've seen it there in the sink many times. And then, it disappeared for months. I guess somebody brought it to the convent? I don't know. So, last Wednesday after dinner, I went to empty the garbage in the large bin outside, and I saw it in the trash. My son and daughter are four and seven years old and they love watching old Westerns on TV, so I figured I'd just take it. They're throwing it out anyway."

She stopped, but David looked at her encouragingly, so she kept talking.

"But I saw the stray cat, Louie, so I put some milk in the thermos cup and set it out. A few hours later, I took more trash out to the bin, and the poor kitty is lying next to the milk, dead.

"I felt so sorry for him. I loved that little kitty. I emptied the milk on the ground, asked the gardener to take the cat away, and I put the thermos in a paper bag and set it by the back door to take home later."

"And then I forgot about it. Until I heard on Monday that Sister Anne was poisoned, and I thought about the poor cat and I thought maybe I should tell someone."

She pointed to the thermos. "I don't want it anymore. You keep it. I wonder if it was the same poison that killed the cat and Sister Anne?"

"And you said that the trash goes out Thursday morning?"

"Yes, sir, very early. The garbage truck comes before I come to work."

"So maybe the person who threw it away knew it would be gone before anyone could find it."

Mrs. Huber nodded. "Yes, maybe?"

"Can you think of anyone who might want to harm Sister Anne?"

"I didn't even know her, sir. I don't know. But it's terrible that she was murdered."

"Thank you, Mrs. Huber. And thank you for bringing this thermos. We'll have it tested right away. You did the right thing."

After she left, David carried the paper bag out to his car and got a plastic bag from the trunk.

Could it be this easy? But even if it was the same poison, it still didn't give him the identity of the murderer. But it certainly might narrow it down.

★ ★ ★

David wanted to interview Stacy Richards, Sister Anne's friend. She told David on the phone that she wouldn't be able to help very much, but he got her address and drove to her large ranch-style house about five minutes away from the convent.

All her children were in school, so he sat on the worn couch covered with a beautiful green blanket, and began the interview.

"Mrs. Richards, how well did you know Sister Anne? We heard you spent a lot of time with her in the past three months."

She looked surprised. "That's what Sister Therese asked me last week when she called. I guess Sister Anne told everyone we were friends. But it wasn't true—not at all. I mean, she was nice and everything, but I talked to her only once in September about piano lessons for my son Jake, and he had so many after-school activities that we couldn't fit it in. That's the only time I spoke to her."

"Is there any reason you can think of that some of the sisters thought you and she were best friends?"

"Well, I've been wondering about that all week. Maybe she was meeting someone else and wanted to use me as an excuse. I heard a few days ago that she was pregnant."

David nodded. "Yes, we think that might have been the reason. I still need to ask you what you were doing last Wednesday afternoon."

Stacy thought for a minute. "Last Wednesday? I have no idea. I have five children, three in grade school and two in high school, so I was probably taking one of them somewhere. Paul has judo and Martin is on the football team. I think on Wednesday, I was waiting for Paul at the studio, picked him up, got home, and the kids did their homework before I fixed dinner for everyone. My husband gets home at a little after five o'clock from his construction job."

"Thanks for talking with me. I really appreciate it." David got up. Stacy seemed willing to help, but there wasn't much information she could give him.

★ ★ ★

That evening, I asked David, "You've interviewed everyone. What's next? When do you think we'll get the results from that thermos?"

"I don't know. It'll take a few more days to get that back from the lab. I also have one more interview."

"And no one has claimed to be the father of the child. How will you get that information? No one's going to admit that."

"I know. That's a big problem. But I have a way to rule out a few people. There are some limited tests available—better than a blood test."

"Who are you going to do the tests on?"

"I can't talk about that—yet."

"Okay, I understand."

David and I washed the dishes, fed the cats, and watched a few Christmas programs, but we both felt like going to bed early. He needed to return to the church for another interview, and I needed to practice out there. We would drive separately, though. He didn't want people to know we were a couple, nor did he want me any more involved in this investigation than I already was.

CHAPTER 12

Sister Joan gave David a dirty look as he walked in the front door of the parish office, which he didn't quite understand.

"Sister Joan, could you let Father Michael know that I'm here for another interview? I called him earlier."

Sister Joan hesitantly got up and led him to his office.

David didn't waste any time after he sat down in the two chairs in front of Father Michael's desk.

"Father Michael, we have to find out who is the father of Sister Anne's child. We are able to do some limited paternity testing, so we hope you'll be completely honest with us. I'll be blunt. Are you the father?"

"I know you need to ask these questions, and I understand, but I can assure you that I'm not the father. I'm willing to take any test to prove that. Like I said before, I liked Sister Anne. She was wonderful to work with, but that's all it was—a working relationship. We met to discuss the liturgy and plan the music for Mass, and that was it. I'm willing to cooperate with you completely."

"Okay, thank you. I still need you to take an HLA test, though. It's a little more complicated than a blood test. And I'd like to talk to Father John again, if I can."

Father Michael got up quickly. "I'll take you to his office."

They walked down the hall together to Father John's office, where the door was open. Father Michael then returned to his office.

Father John got up from his desk. "More questions?" He smiled. "Please, have a seat. As I mentioned, we're here to help you with anything you need."

"Well, Father, we really need to find out who the father of Sister Anne's child is. If you know anything about that, you have to tell us. Any person she may have been close to, anyone she mentioned to you. And I'll be honest, we need to rule you out as the father. Can we do that? We do have access to HLA testing, so we will test you for that as well."

Father John sat quietly. "The testing is available to find out who the father is? I wasn't aware of that."

David said, "Yes, it's not one hundred percent, but it is around eighty-percent accurate. It's more sophisticated than it was with a blood test even ten years ago."

Father John got up, walked around his desk, closed the office door, and returned to his chair. Sighing, he looked down at the papers on his desk.

"Well, I guess I can't hide it anymore. I'm the father of her child. But I didn't kill her. I loved her, and I would have loved the child and taken care of it. I was going to renounce my vows and marry her. I told her that a few weeks ago, but then... she died, and the child died, and I don't know what I'm going to do. Do you know if it was a boy or a girl?"

"It was a boy," David said softly.

"A boy. That would have been nice."

"You're saying how much you loved her, Father, but you are a prime suspect in this murder investigation. You have a lot to lose by being the father of her child—your priesthood, your whole career—which means you have a very strong motive for her murder."

"I know, but I didn't kill her. I have an alibi. I told you that last time. I was so upset when I found out she had been killed.

And I couldn't tell anyone or even show how upset I was. It was terrible."

"How did your relationship with Sister Anne begin?"

"She had been there for about a month when I walked past her office on my way to the rectory. She called to me, so I stepped inside. She asked if she could set up a counseling appointment. I said, 'Of course.' She came in the next day, and we talked. I guess I can share all this now since she's gone." He paused for a moment, reached over, and grabbed a tissue to wipe his eyes.

"She was having a lot of trouble fitting in at the convent. She didn't want to leave the order yet, but she was very lonely and felt people didn't like her at all. We talked a lot. I had an easy time relating to her, because I've often felt the same way about the priesthood. It can be a very lonely life."

"When she left that day, she hugged me. Well, it had been a long time since anyone showed me any affection at all. We met again the next week, and one thing led to another. We usually met in the rectory or her office in the afternoon. I'm so incredibly sorry it all happened. I was making plans to leave the priesthood and marry her, but now I'm not sure what I'll do. Especially if everyone finds out I'm the father of her child—or would have been," he added.

David found himself feeling so sad for Father John—and for Sister Anne. The lives of a nun and a priest must be very lonely. Then he realized this could all be a ploy to get his sympathy, and that Father John could very well be the murderer. He couldn't let himself be deceived. He simply said, "We'll check out where you were that afternoon, Father. I'll be getting back to you." He got up quickly and left the priest sitting at his desk, staring blankly across its surface.

David went outside to his car. He sat there quietly for a while, gazing at the church and the empty parking lot. The sky was grey, and it looked like it might snow later in the day. He really wanted to talk to Kristen. He was so glad she had been kicked out of the convent and that they had gotten together. He couldn't imagine a lonelier life than that of a priest or nun. Surrounded by people, but without anyone who truly loved you, with no one to spend the rest of your life with.

He was being ridiculous. Most marriages weren't that great. His parents had divorced early in his life, and there hadn't been any love there. Finding someone and falling in love wasn't always the solution to loneliness. It might work for a while, but love faded and ended so frequently. He wondered if he and Kristen had a chance at lasting love or if it would end badly.

He didn't want to think about it anymore. He glanced at his watch and headed back to the station.

CHAPTER 13

I was bored. My grades should have come in the mail by now. I was sure I had passed, but I needed confirmation before I could celebrate. David couldn't share very much about his interviews. He offered me a few snippets, but most of it was off-limits to me, making our dinner conversations quieter and quieter. He did tell me about the thermos and the cat, though. We talked that evening over our grilled-cheese sandwiches. I opened a can of green beans to get our almost-fresh vegetable with the meal.

He lifted the sandwich to his mouth, then put it back down. "You know, I'm sure glad you got kicked out."

I laughed. "What do you mean?"

"Well, after interviewing the nuns and priests out there, I realize that a lot of them are really lonely. There aren't enough people there to be their friends, and they don't have anyone who really loves them. I feel sorry for them. I'm glad you're not living that life anymore."

He reached across the table, took my hand, and held it tightly.

I was so lucky I had found someone who loved me, and I wished it hadn't taken me so long to realize it.

"But," I began slowly, not sure of what I even wanted to say, "there's a lot to be said for that kind of life for some people. It can be very satisfying."

"You really think so?"

"I do. There were a lot of people in the motherhouse to be friends with. If I had stayed longer, I think some of them could have been lifelong friends. And friendship can be very satisfying."

"But that's different from being in love."

"Yes, but being in love and having children isn't always the most wonderful experience, either. Consider the divorce rates and the unhappy marriages that don't necessarily end in divorce."

"That's true. I have my parents as an example of that." he said sadly.

"And not having a family enables priests and nuns to devote their lives to helping other people. I know a lot of them don't seem to do that, but some do. There are some amazing priests and nuns who spend their entire lives helping others in orphanages or schools, or out on missions. They couldn't do that and take care of a family."

"Well, the priests and nuns out at St. Boniface don't seem to be doing much with their lives except having a lot of regrets."

"I feel sorry for them." I meant it. "Did you find out any more information you can share with me?"

"No, not really. But let me know what it's like out there when you go to practice this week. I sure wish you hadn't promised Sister Anne that you'd help her."

"I know. And Christmas is the hardest time of the year. I really need to practice. She was so good at the organ, but I'm not. I'll do my best."

I didn't want to think about the services coming up in the next few weeks, so we started talking about what we could get my parents for Christmas.

* * *

Before I went to sleep that night, I lay awake for a long time, thinking about what David and I had talked about. I heard him gently breathing next to me and realized again how lucky I was to have his love. But there were many sisters and I supposed priests also, though I didn't know very many, who were happy and well-adjusted people who loved their lives. That was the reason I had entered the convent. I had known some of them and admired their lives and how committed they were to helping others. I wanted to be like that. They had friends and companionship, and didn't seem to be lacking anything.

But there were many others who'd had a more difficult time. Especially in the smaller missions where there wasn't much choice of friends. My convent friends were all out on mission. Sometimes they would get assigned to large missions, but often there would be only three nuns. An elderly sister, the principal or superior, and a young one who had just graduated. It could be horribly lonely. I was glad I was gone. You never knew where you might end up.

CHAPTER 14

David went back the next day to interview Sister Therese.

"Sister Therese, I need to know why you lied to us in the last interview about Sister Anne's pregnancy. You told me you had no idea she was pregnant. But that's not true, is it?"

Sister Therese looked at David for a few seconds. "No. I lied. I'm sorry, but I was so upset about it."

David was blunt. "Lying to the police in a murder investigation doesn't look good for you. Plus, it's a crime."

"I know, I know. It's just that ever since she told us about her pregnancy, I've been so angry. I've tried to be a good leader for this little community, but everyone seems to hate me. Everyone has their little secrets and talks to each other, but no one ever talks to me. I knew Sister Anne was having trouble. I knew she was lonely and upset; even Sister Frances hates it here. I've tried. I really have. And then Sister Anne gets pregnant. Now that's on my record too—allowing that to happen. I'm so angry about everything."

"Angry enough to poison Sister Anne?"

"No, of course not. It couldn't have been any of us."

"We're not sure of the exact time of death, Sister."

"What do you mean, you're not sure? You told me last week that her watch read two thirty or something, and that's how you knew. And now you're changing your story? Why? Are you trying to pin her murder on one of us? I thought you people knew what you were doing."

"Yes, we know what we're doing, and what we're doing is trying to narrow the list of suspects."

"Well, I was angry with her, but I didn't kill her. You might not think very much of us, but we are a good, dedicated group of educators trying to improve people's lives, not harm them."

David ignored the remark. "What did you do after school that afternoon?"

"I finished up in the office and came back here and read in this room."

"Did Sister Frances know you had come back?"

"No, why would she? She was probably in the kitchen preparing dinner. I don't report where I'm going every minute of the day."

"You have a very strong motive for wanting to get rid of Sister Anne. It would have solved a lot of problems for you."

"Well, it didn't solve anything, did it? Now she's dead, and the whole world knows she was pregnant. Instead of being a quiet thing that could have been hushed up, now it's in the newspapers. No, believe me, she was going to quietly leave the order and have the baby, and that would have done it. There was no reason for anyone to kill her."

"I think that's enough for today," David said abruptly.

He got up. Sister Therese appeared shocked that he would leave so quickly. She got up from her desk but didn't say anything.

★ ★ ★

David had finished all his interviews, but without a clear idea of who had killed Anne. He was waiting on the report from the thermos, but that wouldn't help narrow down the suspects. He hoped Father John's confession hadn't been a ploy to get him out of a murder. He needed to leave the priesthood. He would be a lot happier somewhere else. But where? It would be difficult to leave something you've worked your whole life to achieve.

This investigation seemed to be at a standstill, like so many of them. David's investigations usually followed a pattern. He would get a lot of information, become frustrated, and then weeks or even months later, there would be some new information that would break the case and lead directly to a solution. He hoped the solution would be fast in this case. Especially for Kristen's sake. And his too. He'd like to wrap this up before Christmas. The word "wrap" brought a smile to his face. He needed to get something for Kristen, but he couldn't even imagine what that might be. Did other men have the same problems with their wives and girlfriends? He thought so. She didn't like perfume and she didn't wear much jewelry. But maybe that was because she didn't have any. Maybe he should surprise her with some. It was as confusing as trying to figure out a murder. Maybe he should ask her.

He looked at his watch. Five thirty. He was anxious to get home and talk to Kristen. Not that he could tell her much about the investigation. He certainly couldn't tell her that Father John had confessed to being the father of the child.

CHAPTER 15

The traffic was light, and I arrived at the church quickly. I got the key from Sister Joan, who seemed friendlier than before—maybe because I was doing everyone a favor by playing for the Christmas Masses. I couldn't quite tell. I walked down the corridor and into the side door of the dim church. The choir door was locked and I used the key and turned on the light. I wondered again at the landing about the large window that let useless light into the stairwell as I turned and walked up to the choir loft.

I had set the music by the organ from the choir practice the other evening, so it was right there on the organ bench. I took off my heels and put on my organ shoes so I could play the pedals. However, as I sat on the bench and turned on the organ, I felt dizzy. I must have been the first person to play it since Sister Anne was murdered. I glanced around the loft, fully expecting to see someone come for me. I tried to concentrate on the music, but it was hard to focus. My thoughts kept going back to Anne and how she had been so talented, and what a huge loss her life had been. How could someone have taken her life? And why? She had her whole life ahead of her. And not only her life, but the life of her unborn child. I got through everything I had to play, but it was a struggle. I had another week to practice, though. I turned off the organ, left the music on the organ bench, and hurried down the steps.

I had Christmas presents to think about. I needed to get David something, and I had to buy presents for my parents. I finally could afford to buy real presents instead of the home-made jam and handwritten cards like I had given my entire life. The money I had from the *Silent Night* manuscript enabled me to be like an adult for the first time in my life. I didn't know what to buy anyone, though. I stopped at the mall on my way home, but nothing was very appealing. David didn't need clothes or shoes or power tools or liquor or any of the things that girls got guys for Christmas. I left without buying a thing. I felt like our love was the best gift of all, and we had both received that already.

My parents called and invited us for Christmas dinner. I told them I'd have to check with David, but I was sure it would be fine.

★ ★ ★

I had very little time left. It was the week before Christmas, with only one more practice. I went to practice Wednesday afternoon and I'd meet with the choir for the last time on Thursday. David was in the office all day. He had finished his interviews. No one knew we were even acquainted.

Practicing was a little easier this time. I put her murder out of my mind and tried to focus on the music. I think it was easier because I had to perfect the pieces in only a few days, which scared me and made me concentrate.

After a while, I heard a noise and looked over at the stairs. Sister Joan walked toward me.

"Hi," I said, puzzled.

"Hello. How's it going?"

"I'm almost finished."

"Can I sit down?"

"Sure," I answered. I had just seen her when I came into the office. I wondered why she had come up here.

"I wanted to clear up a few things that have been bothering me."

"Oh," I replied, wondering what was wrong. I couldn't even imagine.

"I was wondering how you were getting along with Father Michael. You've met with him a few times about the liturgy, haven't you?"

I was confused. Why would she care about how I was getting along with Father Michael? But I decided to be honest. There wasn't any harm in that.

"Well, I've only met with him a few times, helping out with the liturgy. He was the one who told me I should go to choir practice, and that I'd get a good idea of what Sister Anne was doing for the Masses. He didn't know. And then I met with him to tell him what Sister Anne had planned. He seems very nice," I added at the end. I couldn't think of anything else to tell her—or that I wanted to tell her.

"Well, you've seen that detective that's been coming around here after the accident?"

She had no idea that David and I were a couple; she didn't even know we knew each other. I wasn't going to let her know otherwise, but figured I'd let her do the talking.

"Yeah, I saw some police when I was here last week."

She continued quickly. "I think that detective has a lot of nerve, interviewing the priests over and over. They both have solid alibis for the time of the murder, and he keeps after them like they're guilty. He doesn't know anything about being Catholic, or about nuns or priests. Those men are representatives of God here on Earth, and it's disgusting the way he's bombarding them with questions and insinuations. They had absolutely nothing to do with her death."

I couldn't believe how angry she was. Such an archaic, patriarchal idea.

I barely managed to say, "Oh," before she continued to rant. But I also knew from experience that priests were human, like anyone else. If only she knew what I knew about them. If I'd learned one thing helping David with the three murder cases, it was that everyone, even priests and nuns, were as capable as anyone else of deceit, jealousy, and even murder.

"I know. Trust me, I know." She was almost yelling. "I work with them every single day, and I know them better than almost anyone else. They are both incapable of doing anything bad."

"This is a murder investigation, Sister. I'm sure that as a policeman, he needs to ask these questions."

"And they should be looking for the real killer—the father of that child."

She sat there quietly, looking at me.

"I should probably practice a little more," I said.

She blinked, almost as if she had just come out of a trance. Her anger wasn't directed toward me, but at David, and I had nothing to do with him or the investigation. She just needed someone to vent to.

"I'm sorry. I'll let you finish practicing. Let me know when you leave."

"Okay, I'll probably be back again in the next few days, and for choir practice this Thursday."

She got up and headed to the stairs. She glanced back at me once, then disappeared down the steps.

It was such a strange encounter, I wasn't sure what to make of it. She seemed very concerned with my thoughts about Father Michael, not Father John. And she was so angry at David. I'd have to tell him what she said. I really tried to stay out of this murder—I really did. Why I kept getting dragged into these investigations, I didn't know. This was definitely the last one. I meant it this time.

★ ★ ★

I picked up a pizza from our Italian restaurant for dinner. I didn't even bother to ask David because he'd be fine with it. He didn't care much about food. Whatever was on his plate was fine. Whether it was a fancy salmon dish, an Italian pasta, or something from Steak and Shake, it was all the same to him.

He walked in the door after six.

"Hey, how was your day?"

I was petting both cats on the couch and reading *A Christmas Carol* by Dickens, since it was a story I loved and it was only ten days before Christmas.

"Hi. It was fine. I got us Hawaiian pizza for dinner. I hope that's okay."

"Are you kidding? It sounds wonderful. Do we have any Cokes?"

"Of course. Let me fix dinner. It's really difficult. You'd better take over the petting." I laughed as I put two slices of pizza on a plate for him.

He sat next to me for a few minutes, but the cats weren't pleased at being displaced.

"I think we'll have to wait for a while before we can eat." He smiled.

"We know who's the most important, don't we?" I agreed.

Eventually we reheated the pizza, and as we sat on the couch eating, I told him about the encounter with Sister Joan in the choir loft.

"That's why she gave me such a dirty look yesterday when I came to talk to Father John and Father Michael," he said.

"I'm sure that was it. She was angry that you would even consider them as suspects."

"She doesn't know that we know each other, does she?"

"No, and I don't want her to find out. That would likely make her even angrier, though I'm not sure why."

"I'm done with their investigations, at least for the time being. I hope she doesn't bother you anymore."

"Yeah, me too. I want to play these Masses and get out of there. Oh, by the way, my parents invited us for Christmas dinner. Do you think you can make it?"

"Let me check my schedule. I hope I'm off on Christmas. And it would be wonderful to see them again. It's been way too long. I miss them."

"They miss you! They're so excited we're back together."

"They know we're living together?" he asked.

"Yes, and that's how much they like you. They even think that's okay. You're Irish and a policeman. What more could they ask for?"

"I agree with them. What more could you possibly want?"

"If they only knew what you were really like!"

"And what does *that* mean?"

I attempted to frown, but he kissed me, and I completely forgot what I had been teasing him about. Even though the cats had hopped back on the couch, they eventually grew tired of being ignored and slid off one by one to do their own thing.

CHAPTER 16

I went to our last choir practice before Christmas on Thursday night. I wasn't ready, but the choir sounded good. I needed to get in the church a few more times to go over all the music. Every time I thought about playing the Masses, I almost had a panic attack. Why did I ever say yes to this? I must have been out of my mind.

I finally got my grades from my final exams and I'd passed everything. I had my degree and would be able to apply for a teaching job next semester—not in the spring, it was too late for that. And I still had to complete my semester of practice teaching. But I might actually be a teacher next fall. I was excited about that. I hoped I could get a job. But I had to play these stupid services first. I certainly didn't want to be a music director. I hoped they found someone soon.

* * *

On Friday, I went upstairs to the freezing choir loft, thinking they would attract more Catholics if they heated the church. I was glad I brought my sweater, but it wasn't even enough to keep me from shivering while I played.

I heard the door to the choir loft open and close. I saw someone appear at the door to the loft. Sister Joan again. Oh, God. I didn't want to see her. I didn't have time to listen to her complain about something I had nothing to do with. And I didn't have anything to do with this investigation. As far as she knew, I was here because Sister Anne asked me to play for a few Masses. That was it.

"I saw you going to Father Michael's office."

Well, that was blunt. What was it with her and Father Michael? Did she have a problem with him?

"Yes, I told him what we were doing for the Christmas liturgies to make sure they were all right with him."

"Has he been up here to the choir loft?"

"No, I haven't seen him. Why are you asking me all these questions about Father Michael?"

She walked closer to the organ and put her hand on it. "I've seen the way you look at him. He's quite handsome, isn't he?"

I stared at her. "Honestly, I didn't notice. I'm engaged to a wonderful man, and I'm not interested in looking at other men, especially priests."

"You know he'll never feel the same way about you as he did about Anne, right?"

I would have edged away from her, but I couldn't, since I was on the organ bench. All I wanted to do was get out of the loft—and the church. She was crazy. I wasn't sure what she was going to do next.

"She was going to have his baby. So don't think he'll ever be interested in you. He's come to me to talk everything over with me. You're nothing to him."

"Listen," I said quickly, "I'd better be going."

"No, no, I'll go. You stay and finish practicing." She turned abruptly and started down the choir loft stairs. I heard her go all the way to the bottom of the stairs and then the door closed. Thank God.

I started to practice again, mostly for something to do. I didn't want to leave while she was still in the church, but I couldn't concentrate on the music. I played for about fifteen minutes, then called it quits. It was about four thirty and it was already starting to get dark. I had to get home and tell David about this latest crazy development.

I turned off the organ, changed my shoes, and left the music on the organ bench. Why would Sister Joan think I was interested in Father Michael? And then I realized. She was jealous. She must have been jealous for a long time, especially if she thought he loved Anne and didn't care for her. And if she thought he was the father of Anne's child? Oh, God, she could have killed Anne. I didn't want to be anywhere near her again. I didn't want to be alone with her. I'd have to come back tomorrow, but I needed someone to go with me. I didn't want another encounter with Sister Joan.

I glanced down at the church below. It was getting dark and even gloomier. There were no lights on at all. When I turned off the lights in the choir loft, it would be almost black. I needed to get out of there fast.

I slowly walked to the steps and opened the door. Even before I opened it, I had the horrible feeling she would be standing there waiting, but I still wasn't prepared for the suddenness and ferocity of the attack. She grabbed my arm, tripped me by putting her leg out, and pushed me hard.

I didn't even have time to grab hold of the wooden banister as I pushed my purse into her face and tumbled down the ten steps to the landing.

All I could feel was the excruciating pain in my leg. It was bent at a horrific angle, and I saw the bone sticking out of it. I must have passed out, because when I woke up, the church was dark and silent, and I couldn't move. I felt for my purse and found it. I had a small flashlight in it (David had insisted on it) and I pulled it out and turned it on to look at my leg. I could see the bone, and blood around the wound and on the tile beside it. I felt like throwing up when I looked at it. I had to get out of here somehow. I tried to carefully move my leg, but the pain was too much. I almost passed out again, so I lay back against the cold wall and tried not to lose consciousness.

I shone the flashlight down the remaining steps to the choir loft door at the bottom of the steps. There were at least twenty steps. I couldn't even move at all. There was no way I could navigate those steps with my leg broken like it was. But I couldn't just stay here all night. What a stupid thing I had done. No one knew where I was. People knew I had been here practicing, but everyone would assume I had gone home. All the lights were off, and the doors were closed.

David would have gotten home and would be wondering what had happened to me, but he wouldn't have any idea I had gone to practice. I could have been at my parents,' or shopping for Christmas presents or getting food for dinner or anything. I didn't usually tell him where I was going during the day.

What would David do if I didn't come home? He had no way of reaching me. No one at the convent knew I was here. No one at the church, or the priests, knew I was still here. The only person who knew was Sister Joan, and she wasn't going to tell anyone. Why did she leave me here? Why didn't she come back to finish the job? I knew now that she had killed Sister Anne, and she knew I knew, so why did she leave me here? Unless she was sure I would be dead by morning. That was a sobering thought. And entirely possible. The church was freezing and I was injured.

I wondered if I would make it until morning. I couldn't really tell the extent of my injuries, but I had to do something. I had to at least elevate my leg. I tore off a piece of cloth from my ruined pants. I tried to tie it above where the bone was sticking out to prevent any more blood loss. Better to do it while I still could. I tried to move, and each motion was almost enough to make me throw up, but I finally managed to hoist my broken leg up on a step so it would be elevated. I drifted in and out of consciousness. It wasn't sleep. When I was awake, I thought of all the stupid things I had done in my short life. If I was still alive in the morning, I would tell David I wanted to marry him. I would call Mom and Dad more often. I had been neglecting them for months. I would sit and pet JC every night and hold him and tell him how much I loved him. I would never complain about anything again—ever.

Then I would jolt awake in the darkness. I couldn't fall asleep because I would freeze. The temperature must be below thirty degrees in the church. I could see my watch, but strangely enough, it was cracked like Sister Anne's. What a bizarre coincidence—strange and awful.

Hours went by. I planned my funeral; not that it would do any good. I should have worried about Sister Joan coming back to kill me, but strangely enough I didn't worry about that. Between the pain, I planned the rest of my life, just in case. I would get my teaching job very soon. I thought of my life with David. I wondered if we would have children. I never even asked him if he wanted to have children. I didn't know if I wanted any. I didn't think I did, but maybe it might be nice if we had a few. His parents didn't like him very much, so maybe he wouldn't want children. I'd have to ask him.

I wasn't afraid of the dark. That was a good thing. I remembered when I was worried about the killer that first year when I thought they were coming to kill me. She wouldn't dare come back to the church. That gave me some peace of mind. I don't remember much else, except that I was very cold. I drifted in and out of consciousness. It must have been hours. I would wake up suddenly and not remember where I was, but then I would remember the pain.

CHAPTER 17

I heard voices. They were distant. It couldn't be Joan. She would come back alone, not talking to anyone. I tried to yell, but all I could manage was a worthless moan. I tried again. This time I screamed.

Then I heard the voices get nearer, and running on the tile. I heard the key turn in the door and the light blinded me. David was there with the two priests.

"Oh, my God, Kristen!" He ran up the steps and turned quickly. "Call an ambulance!"

I heard footsteps running away. I could see his face over mine. He covered me quickly with his jacket.

"I'm so glad you found me."

"What are you doing here? What happened?"

"Sister Joan."

He held me in his arms and I didn't say another word.

The next thing I remembered was the pain as they lifted me carefully onto the stretcher. Before I passed out again, I grabbed David's arm. "Sister Joan. I think she killed Anne."

"I know," he said. "And you're going to be okay."

★ ★ ★

I remembered waking up like this before. A hospital room. The windows. The IV drip in my arm. I felt my head. There were no bandages. That must have been a different time. But my leg was numb and heavy. I saw David and my parents start to stand up.

"This has happened before," I said stupidly. It was all I could think of to say.

David took my hand. "Yes, but this'll be the last time it happens. And you'll be glad to know that Sister Joan is in jail."

"Who?" I asked.

My mom stood by the side of the bed. "How are you feeling, hon?"

"Okay, I guess." I was a little groggy, but nothing hurt. I think my leg would have hurt, but I probably had a lot of medication in me. I looked at David. "I'm so glad you found me. How did you find me?"

"Well, you know how we've been using your car to come out here for the interviews? Father Michael's been thinking about getting a new car. He noticed your Duster the last few times you were at the church, and then yesterday, while locking up the church, he saw it was the only car in the parking lot. It was the same color, and he wondered what it was doing there. He saw a Washington University sticker on the back window and realized it belonged to you. He went into the church and called your name, but there was no answer. He returned to the rectory and called my station, and they got in touch with me. He asked if you had come home, and at that point, I was frantic, so I drove right out here. That's when we went into the church and heard you."

"I was so afraid you wouldn't hear me."

"It certainly got our attention."

"That was the whole point. My leg?" I asked fearfully.

"It's broken badly below the knee, but they reset it and it'll be in a cast for six weeks, but it should heal up okay. You're very lucky you didn't bleed more."

"How long do you think I'll be in here?"

My mom answered that one. "Dr. Ward said maybe a week, but you have to rest and take it easy."

I turned my head to David. "Have you talked to Sister Joan yet?"

"No, not yet."

"Well, I want to be there when you do. I'll get out of here as soon as I can."

"Not until you talk to the doctor, you won't."

"Okay, okay, but I hope I can be there. You won't believe the things she said to me up in the choir loft."

"Rest now. We can talk about this later. Go back to sleep. You're safe now. Just rest."

I looked at my parents, sitting with worried looks on their faces. I smiled at them as best I could.

"Don't worry. I'm going to be fine." I closed my eyes. I couldn't keep them open anymore.

★ ★ ★

I felt so much better the next few days that I was ready to get up and leave. The therapist came in and helped me walk with the cast and crutches. I could do this. I still had enough medication in me that I didn't feel much pain at all.

David was anxious for me to get out of the hospital but made it very clear that he would be interrogating Sister Joan on his own. "Don't worry. I'll get all the information I need from you. I'll be able to handle her. When you get out of here, you need to go home and rest. Let me do my job."

In the next few days, I told David everything she had said and done in the choir loft, along with her strange obsession with Father Michael. He was one of my visitors on the third day. He was very kind and considerate, expressing his regret that I couldn't play for the Christmas liturgies. He mentioned they had hired a substitute and hoped the man would work out. Although he didn't seem to know the liturgy as well as I did, Father Michael remained optimistic.

Father John also came to visit. He was quieter but appeared thoughtful, sincerely regretting that he hadn't recognized Sister Joan's problems sooner.

By the fifth day, the twenty-seventh of December, I could hardly wait until the doctor came in for his morning rounds. I was anxious to get out of there. I had missed Christmas and I was feeling bad about that. I also wanted to hear what David had to say when he interviewed Sister Joan.

The doctor told me I could leave, and the nurse came in later with the discharge papers to sign. One of the nuns, Sister Claire, called and told me the substitute did a terrible job playing the Masses and they were sorry I hadn't been there. I felt bad that I had missed Christmas with David and my parents, but they promised we would celebrate it in early January with dinner and presents and it would be the same, only a different date.

David helped me with my crutches and small suitcase, and I managed to get in the car. As we drove away from the hospital, David asked, "Remember the last time I picked you up from the hospital?"

"How could I forget?"

That was when he'd held my hand for the first time all the way back to the motherhouse and gave me my first real kiss.

"We can have a repeat of that, you know." He smiled.

"I know. But it's not the same as the first time."

"That's because you're spoiled now. You expect so much more."

"You're right." I leaned over to him. "And I'd better get it."

"Oh, don't worry, you will. But I think you need to rest."

I laughed. "I'm so tired of resting. You have no idea."

"Well, I'll put you to bed anyway," he said. "Sounds perfect."

I was looking forward to a few months with no classes, nuns, priests, or anything connected to my old life.

"You know how I said I was done with all things related to the church? Well, I really mean it this time."

"I'm going to hold you to that," David said. "I don't care who you used to know, or what story they tell you. Don't fall for it. You're finished. For good."

"Yes, I swear. No more convents. No more convent murders!"

"Thank God for that."

I laughed. "I thought you didn't believe in God."

"I don't, but if he or she can keep you out of more trouble, I might reconsider."

I smiled. "Well, I hope He or She does just that."

CHAPTER 18

David walked into the interview room where Sister Joan was sitting.

"Sister Joan, I need to ask you a few more questions about last week, and about Sister Anne's murder. I'm recording this interview."

She looked up at him and folded her hands neatly on the table in front of her.

"Why don't you tell me what happened last week when you met Kristen in the choir loft?" David asked.

"I already told the other policeman. I don't know why I have to go through this again."

David repeated the question. "Why did you go up to the choir loft?"

"I went up there to let her know that Sister Therese wanted to see her. That was the only reason."

"And what happened when you were up there?"

"What do you mean? I told her that Sister Therese needed to see her, and then I left."

"Did you say anything else to Kristen?"

"I might have mentioned her jealousy about Father Michael. She couldn't keep her eyes off him. And he's a priest! It was disgusting, the way she acted. She was so jealous."

"Jealous? Of whom?"

"Well, of me. My relationship with Father Michael. We're such good friends, and now that Sister Anne is gone, he's been turning to me for comfort. He was romantically involved with her. She seduced him, of course, and she was having his baby. But he didn't really love her. He told me that often."

"So even though Kristen had only been there twice to go through some music, she was jealous of you already?"

"Yes, I've seen the way she's looked at him."

"Thank you, Sister. I have another question for you."

He reached down, opened his briefcase, and put the old thermos on the table.

She stared at it. Her skin got even paler than its pasty white, and she didn't say a word.

"I'll bet you didn't think you'd ever see that again, did you?"

"I don't know what you're talking about."

"I'll tell you then, Sister. This thermos contained the poison that killed Sister Anne—and her and your fingerprints are all over it."

"Where did you get that?"

David said, "I think you know where I got it. But why did you throw it in the trash? Was it because you knew it would go out in the morning?"

"I have absolutely no idea what you're talking about. Sister Anne used that thermos. Plenty of people used it. It was in the staff lunchroom for a while. Everybody saw it there. I never threw it anywhere. I used it maybe once, a few months ago. That's why my fingerprints are on it."

"Why are yours and Sister Anne's the only fingerprints on it?"

"I have no idea. You're the investigator. You tell me!"

David said calmly, "I think you need to tell me, Sister. We have all the time in the world."

Sister Joan was silent.

"All right, let's talk about what Kristen has testified, about how you pushed her down the choir loft steps."

"I didn't do anything like that! I left the choir loft while Kristen was still practicing the organ. What happened after that, I have no idea. She probably fell down the steps, but I had nothing to do with that."

"You've been arrested and held because of the testimony of Kristen, who has said very clearly that it was you who pushed her down the steps and would have left her there all night."

"And of course you believe her! Why don't you believe me? You think you know everything, don't you?"

"No, I don't," David said. "Why don't you fill us in on the rest?"

"I don't have anything to fill in. I didn't do anything to anyone."

"Were you jealous of Sister Anne and Father Michael?"

"Of course I was. He was the one who got her pregnant. He was a foolish man. He's been confiding in me since she's gone. We're much closer now that she's gone."

"Did you think he was the father of her baby?"

"Of course he was. I saw the way they looked at each other in the parish office. And it would have been so easy for them to get together almost every day in her office. It wasn't his fault, though. She was the one who seduced him."

"It sounds as if you wanted to get rid of her so you could have him all to yourself."

"Of course not. He's a priest. I respect that. I would never think of him that way. She didn't respect him at all, obviously."

"Why does this thermos have your fingerprints all over it? And hers?"

"Okay, I did bring her hot chocolate that day, but it was good hot chocolate, fixed the way she liked it. I had some too. I left it there with her and went back downstairs to my office and worked. I didn't hear anything from the choir loft and the light was still on, so I went up there and she was lying on the wooden pew. I couldn't wake her up. I felt for a pulse. There wasn't any. I guess I panicked. I took the thermos and left quickly. I threw it out. I figured she had probably put some poison in it and killed herself. I would have done the same thing if I had found out I was pregnant. But I didn't want to be blamed for her death, so I didn't say anything to anybody. I didn't know that somebody was going to take it out of the trash. I had no idea at the time that there was even any poison in it."

She paused. "Who got it out of the trash?" she almost whispered.

"Mrs. Huber, who was about to bring it home to her children, who would have been poisoned too. The parish cat was poisoned also. I'll bet you didn't want to poison them, did you? You just wanted to poison Sister Anne."

Sister Joan looked out the window and was silent for a few minutes. David sat there patiently before he continued.

"You left her body there on the pew, didn't tell a soul, and disposed of what might have been the cause of her death?"

"I was afraid everyone would blame me. You know they would have!"

"She could have died of a heart attack or a stroke, if what you're telling me is true. You took the thermos because you knew how she died, didn't you, Sister?"

"I thought she might have poisoned herself. I would have killed myself, if I had gotten into that situation with Father Michael. He would never have left the priesthood for her. Ever! And she knew that."

"Father John was actually the father of her child," David said simply.

"What? No, that's impossible. It was Father Michael. I saw the way she looked at him and acted around him. She practically threw herself at him. Nobody cares about Father John. Who would want him? You're wrong. You're completely wrong."

"Father John was the father of her child."

She smiled suddenly. "It wasn't Michael?" She sat very quietly. Then she said, "I'm glad about that. That means he'll be staying here as a priest." Then she stopped. Her face got very pale, and she looked down at the table.

"I did all that for nothing, then, didn't I?"

David didn't say anything for a long time before finally saying, "Yes, you did." He waited a few seconds. "So tell me what really happened, Sister."

Joan started talking quickly and quietly.

"She was a slut. She was out to get Father Michael as soon as she met him. And I saw them go into her office every week to work on the liturgy. I wondered what they did in there. And then we found out she was pregnant. I was so disgusted with her."

"Didn't you blame the man who got her pregnant?" David asked.

"No, she had her plans." She kept talking. "Father Michael would have had to leave the priesthood and his whole life would have been ruined, just because of one stupid mistake. I couldn't bear the thought of him leaving. It broke my heart. And she was so proud and arrogant. She thought she was special because she played the organ so well. Everyone told her how amazing she was. It was disgusting. There are a lot of us who work just as hard and long and nobody thanks us—ever! It isn't fair."

She paused for a minute and closed her eyes. "Last Tuesday I went to the church when she was supposed to be practicing, but she was nowhere to be found. I knew she was with him. Father John was in his office, but Father Michael was gone with her somewhere. I had to do something—and I had to do it fast. So the next afternoon, I grabbed that old thermos, made hot chocolate in the staff room, added the poison—"

"Where did you get the poison, sister?"

"I knew where the gardener kept all his supplies—locked up in the supply room outside—so I got it from there. He was gone on Tuesday, the day I got it."

"And then what did you do?"

"I took it to her. She thought it was strange. I obviously didn't like her, and here I was, giving her a drink she loved. But she took it and we talked a little as she drank it. She started to play another piece, but then she collapsed and I left her there. I checked her pulse to make sure and wiped everything down before I left. I reset her watch to two thirty so Jennifer in the office would be able to say I had been working at that time."

David watched Sister Joan for any sign of anguish or remorse for what she had done, but he didn't see any at all.

"I threw the thermos in the trash. I knew the trash collectors came early in the morning, and it would be gone. I don't know how Mrs. Huber even saw it in the bin. She wasn't supposed to."

She closed her eyes. "I would have gotten away with the whole thing if it hadn't been for her, wouldn't I?" She looked at David, waiting for a reply.

"Well, we'll never know, will we, Sister?" David said sadly.

CHAPTER 19

David came home from work. I was so glad to see him. Not only because my leg ached and it was difficult to get around the apartment, but also because it was wonderful to see him.

He picked up a pizza on the way home. I was starving. We sat on the couch. I started to eat my Hawaiian half while David took a slice from his "everything" half.

"I can share some of what Sister Joan said in the interrogation today, if you're interested."

I kept eating, taking a drink of Dr. Pepper.

He was quiet.

"Of course I'm interested, silly. Tell me what she said."

"I was hoping you'd ask." He smiled. "She denied everything at first, then she claimed she had brought hot chocolate to Anne, insisting it didn't contain any poison at all. She resented the idea that Father Michael and Sister Anne were together, even though they weren't. In her deluded mind, she was the one Father Michael was madly in love with, and they met whenever possible. She was completely shocked when I informed her that Father John was the father of Sister Anne's baby."

Kristen confirmed what David was saying. "She thought I was in love with Father Michael too. I had only met him once or twice, yet she was convinced I was crazy about him. I couldn't believe it."

"She denied pushing you down the steps. She said you were still practicing when she left, and that you must have tripped and fallen when you went down the steps later."

"Wow, she really is crazy."

"No, she just doesn't want to be accused of murder and attempted murder and serve a long jail sentence. She's trying really hard, but I don't think it's going to work. Your testimony is crucial."

"I wonder why she didn't come back and finish me off. Then she could have said that I fell down the choir loft stairs and no one would have ever known the truth."

"You're lucky she didn't. I have no idea why she didn't. It would have been much smarter for her to have killed you."

I shuddered at the thought.

David moved closer and held me tightly. "I didn't mean that the way it sounded. But it would have been smarter for her. I'm certainly glad she wasn't that smart. I love having you around."

He kissed me. I didn't know why I had been so lucky, but I was. First of all, to have found him, and to have escaped death not only once, but twice. I was truly a blessed person.

I thought about all the people I had met this past week. I had no sympathy for Sister Joan. Well, maybe a little. She was a lonely, delusional, and sad person. But she also was a cold-blooded murderer, and all out of jealousy. Sister Anne might have made a poor judgment call by being with Father John, but I thought he was sincere in wanting to leave the priesthood to take care of her and the child.

Father Michael seemed to be a kind, caring priest who wanted to help others. I hoped he would continue with his vocation and not be affected by all the problems of the past year in the parish.

I felt sorry for all the nuns at the convent. What a sad place to live. I thanked God that I had escaped that life, from living with people who had no idea what community even meant. And some of my classmates were already discovering that out on mission. It could be a very lonely life.

The kitties didn't understand about my leg or the crutches, and they didn't give me any rest as they crawled over me on the couch, sniffing at the pizza. David fed them after we finished eating.

I wondered what kind of sentence Sister Joan would receive for the murder of Sister Anne, and for my attempted murder. I imagined it would be severe.

I put my leg up on the couch and looked at my piano, wondering how difficult it would be to play with my leg in a cast. It was my right leg, but Bach didn't need any pedaling. I figured I would wait a few more days. David stayed close to me and the cats settled down. JC sniffed the crust of pizza and wrinkled his nose. I leaned against David. We were both pretty tired.

I thought about the night I had spent on the steps and how lucky I was that David had found me. That was the second time I had been saved by a priest. Maybe there was something to this prayer thing. And we were so lucky that Mrs. Huber had found the thermos in the trash.

David asked me his usual question. "What are you thinking about?"

"I think I'd like to have some hot chocolate." I started to get up. "Would you like some too?

David looked at me for what seemed like a long time before he answered. "No thanks. Not that I'm worried or anything, but I don't feel like it right now."

I laughed. "I understand completely."

CONVENT MYSTERY # 5

REVENGE

CHAPTER 1

I was only in the hospital for five days after Sister Joan tried to kill me, but I had a lot of time to think. It wasn't that I didn't have visitors. David came by every day after work and sat with me until visiting hours were over. Sometimes I had to tell him to leave because I was too tired and medicated to talk any longer. And honestly, because I couldn't conjure up many interesting stories about my days in the hospital, I knew he was bored. I was the one who usually suggested he leave, get some dinner, and relax at home with the kitties. He had a lot of other activities besides his work. He volunteered with a children's group that the police sponsored, and played tennis with his friends at the public courts in Clayton whenever he got the chance.

I don't think he felt bad about leaving early, even though I appreciated him for coming, and I wasn't sure what I would have done without him.

When I was in the hospital, my parents also visited every day. We talked about David and how I had moved in with him. They didn't mind at all that we weren't married; I think they wondered why it took me so long. They didn't even care that he wasn't Catholic. His being Irish was enough for them. He could do nothing wrong in their eyes. They were still hoping we would get married soon, but if living together was okay with David, it was okay with them. I smiled. My opinions didn't seem to matter much anymore; David's were more important to them.

Because of my hospitalization and slow recovery, I'd missed the cutoff to apply for practice teaching in the spring. I'd have to wait until the fall to finish my credential, even though I hated putting my life off any longer. At least, I had my degree—and my life! I was slowly regaining my health after the "accident," grateful to be alive. I had my two cats. Well, one was technically David's, but we shared them equally.

As I lay in the hospital bed, I realized that my not having been in love before was no reason to keep postponing our marriage. As soon as I got out of the hospital, I would tell David I accepted his proposal and was ready and excited to get married. However, there were a lot of important things to talk about. Children, finances, and his parents and the lack of communication with them. The difference between our families. His goals. Did he want to continue being a detective? Did he want to continue working for the police? I always worried about him getting injured, but I seemed to be the one who ended up in the hospital because of the investigations, not him—investigations in which I had no role. As I lay in the hospital bed with so much time on my hands and nothing to do, I realized there were so many things we had never talked about.

I felt terrible that I couldn't play the Christmas Masses at the church where Sister Anne had worked. The staff and the priests knew what had happened to me, and they knew it had been Sister Joan who'd tried to kill me. The whole congregation knew about it without any announcement. They found a substitute who, I heard, did a terrible job, but there was nothing I could do about it. I felt sorry for whoever had to step in at the last minute. It wasn't easy to be called, especially for one of the biggest liturgies of the year.

★ ★ ★

By January, I needed to do something about my life. I couldn't simply sit around and wait for things to happen. I wanted to practice the piano more, but that wasn't enough to fill up all my time. I could take a few classes toward my master's degree, but I wasn't sure if I was ready to study so soon after finishing my first degree.

One evening, David and I sat at the table, enjoying dinner. I had prepared a mushroom-and-pasta dish that David especially liked.

"I don't know what I'm going to do for these next few months," I said. "I can't start my practice teaching until the fall. I'll try to get it in a public school, unless I could do it in a Catholic school. I think the only requirement is that it needs to be accredited, so maybe I could still start this spring."

"Weren't we just talking about no more churches, nuns, or convent stuff? On the way home from the hospital a few weeks ago?"

"Yes, but I should at least find out about it. I don't want to waste any more time doing nothing."

David got up and poured himself a glass of Dr. Pepper. "You really are hopeless, you know. Would you like something to drink?"

"No, I'll stick with water. I haven't been sleeping that well lately."

A few weeks later, David came in the door after five. I had been practicing, one of the few things I could still do besides reading. However, I was getting bored quickly.

I greeted him with, "Let's go out to dinner!"

He looked tired, but it was unusual that I suggested going out, so he readily agreed.

"Where do you want to go?"

"There's that little Greek restaurant not too far away. Why don't we go there?"

"Okay. I remember we liked it last time."

It was dark and quiet as we sat in the back corner and ordered the shish kebab. After a glass of wine, I said, "I have a reason I asked you out tonight."

"Oh, really? Have you met another nun or priest? Are you in love with him or her and planning to leave me?"

I laughed. "No, that's not it. But it does have to do with vows."

David looked worried. "Oh, no. You want to go back to the convent?"

I laughed. "No! Remember all the times you asked me to marry you?"

"Yeah," he said tentatively.

"Can I say yes, or is it too late?"

He set down his wine, leaned across the small table, and kissed me. "It's not too late. In fact, I think it's the perfect time. I can't believe it!" He was smiling now. "Why did you change your mind?"

I held his hand. "Well, when I was on those steps in the cold and dark, and thought I might die, I realized the worst thing that could happen to me, aside from dying, is that we wouldn't be together. Then I thought about how ridiculous it was to wait any longer when I love you and want to be with you forever."

I could see tears in his eyes.

"That's the most wonderful thing anyone's ever said to me. You know I love you too."

"I know."

"I don't have a ring!" he almost shouted, suddenly horrified.

"I don't care. I kind of sprang this on you without any warning. We can go together and pick out something simple. A small wedding is fine with me, too. I don't want anything fancy."

"Thank God. I don't either. I don't really have family and not too many close friends, so it'll be a small group of people."

"I don't want to invite *all* the nuns and priests from the motherhouse, but a few. In fact, I'd love to have the wedding at the motherhouse if you don't mind."

I saw the terror in his face before he realized I was joking. "Ha. Don't worry. Pam is the only person I'll invite, but I would like Father Steven to officiate at our wedding."

"I'll bet he'll like that."

"I know he would."

"You know, there are lots of things we need to talk about if we're going to get married," he said almost apologetically, not wanting to break the mood.

"I know. It'll be a lot different than what we've been doing."

"Well, in some ways." He smiled. "I've wanted to tell you something for a long time. I should have told you when you got all the money from the manuscript."

"What do you mean?" I was suddenly worried I had missed something important. I hoped it wasn't that he was paying child support or had recently finalized a divorce.

"I have some money that my father left me when he passed away ten years ago. It's about $500,000. You've probably wondered how I could have such a nice apartment and car on my policeman's salary."

"I did wonder a little."

"When we get married, we can combine our money, but only if you want to. Otherwise, we can leave the money in separate accounts. I don't want you to feel obligated to put everything together."

"I trust you completely. I wouldn't be marrying you if I didn't. We can combine accounts or leave them separate. I don't care either way. We should talk to a finance person. I had no idea you had so much."

"I was my parents' only child, and when they got divorced, my father never remarried, but my mother did, and went to Spain with her new husband, where she lives now. My father never forgave her, so he left me everything in his will. He never spent any time with me, even though he lived here in St. Louis, and I was raised by my grandparents. Maybe he thought the money would make up for his neglect. I don't know. I guess I'll never know. But I know that's why I love your family so much. They're the family I never had."

"And now you'll always have them, and they love you. Do you want to have children?" I asked him.

"Yes, I really do. I mean, I know my family was awful, but I still want to have children. I help out in that orphanage once a week, and I love those kids. And now that I've seen how families work and how wonderful they can be, I want children of our own. What about you?"

I frowned. "I never planned on having children at all. When I joined the convent, that was one thing I didn't even care about giving up. I never wanted them, and I still don't."

"Well, this might be a problem. It's not something we can compromise on. We can't have half a child."

"Maybe we should have talked about this sooner." I was beginning to get worried.

"Well, it's a good thing we're talking about it now. I've known couples who are really unhappy because they don't agree on this, and one of them invariably ends up angry."

"So what do we do?"

"I don't know. Let's not talk about it anymore tonight. We can talk about it in a few days, after we've given it a little more thought."

"Okay."

We didn't talk about anything else important. Marriage, finances, and children were enough. Deciding on dessert was our only significant decision after that. But when I went to bed that night, I was anxious. Not only did I have to worry about teaching, but I also wondered if this marriage was truly going to happen. Money didn't concern me at all. It was reassuring to know that together, we'd have plenty to start our lives—and have a lot left over for the future. However, the conversation about children was frustrating. Why had I assumed David wouldn't want any? Probably because he had a troubled family, and I couldn't imagine why he'd want to bring children into the world after his experience. Maybe I didn't know him as well as I thought I did. And that worried me too.

On Sunday, we had dinner with my parents and told them we were finally engaged. They were ecstatic. They had waited a long time for the news because I had put David off for years, but now I knew I loved him.

We did need to talk about a few more important things before we set a date.

I spent a lot of time over the next few weeks contemplating the idea of having children. I didn't dislike kids; I wanted to be a teacher and loved being around children. I just wasn't sure if I wanted to dedicate a significant portion of my life to raising one or two. I had witnessed many families who were unhappy with how their children turned out, as well as children who were dissatisfied with their parents. There were families that struggled to get along—parents and children who didn't communicate. My grandparents had issues with their families back in Ireland that I had heard about all my life. My immediate family was fortunate to get along well, but that wasn't something I took for granted. My family seemed to contrast with most, who often had at least one member at odds with another: arguing, fighting, and disagreeing. I didn't want that for myself. It felt safer to stick with only the two of us and avoid risks. It was the coward's way out, but I didn't have a great track record when it came to understanding people. I wasn't sure if anyone else was any better, but I was afraid of having children. I supposed that was the crux of the matter. I had seen and heard too much already, and I didn't want that additional worry in my life.

David and I spoke about it again a few weeks later. I shared all my fears with him. He, of all people, understood and could relate to family issues. Still, he maintained faith and optimism, believing we would be good, responsible parents. He thought we had a better-than-average chance of our family turning out well, and I had to agree with him. Although life never unfolded the way you expected, even when you considered all the options in advance.

I had a lot to think about, and so did he. We didn't reach a conclusion, but at least we understood each other much better. Religion wasn't very important to me. I didn't mind what he believed in, as long as he was a good, moral person, which he was. He didn't believe in God, yet he was kinder and more caring than most of the people I knew who did believe. I noticed how he treated the cats and everyone he encountered; he was a good person. One evening shortly after we met, a spider ran across the floor. I was about to step on it when he exclaimed, "No!" He grabbed a jar, gently scooped it inside, covered it with a paper towel, and walked out to the balcony to release it. At that moment, I understood that he cared about all living things, and I loved that about him.

I was still Catholic, but in name only. I occasionally attended Mass, but I didn't see any reason to go every week. The rules and regulations that had been a part of my life for so long felt meaningless, and I cared much more about being kind to others and trying to be a good person.

One evening, David asked me to sit on the couch with him and the cats.

"You said you don't want a big wedding, right?"

"Yes, just a few people. And I'd like Father Stephen to marry us. But that's it."

"Well, I was thinking that if we have a small wedding and save money on that, we could use it to buy a nice piano for you instead. The money spent on a wedding will be gone in a day, but if we buy a piano, you'll enjoy it every day for years to come."

I began to cry. I loved the idea. I might finally be able to get the piano I had always wanted.

"You want one of those Steinways? Right?" he asked.

"They're really expensive," I told him.

"I checked them out. We can afford one for you. Let's look next weekend and see if you can find one you like. If we combine our money, we'll have enough."

I hugged him, even though the cats were in the way. "That's the nicest thing anyone has ever done for me. Thank you."

We set the wedding date when my practice teaching was finished: the following December, assuming I could teach in the fall.

CHAPTER 3

A few days later, I called Sister Miriam John, one of my English teachers from the convent that first year. I couldn't call Inez anymore. Sister Miriam John told me she'd check to see if there were any available schools for practice teaching in the fall. The next day, she called back, and I learned I could go through the university to teach at Chesterfield, which was a forty-minute drive from where we lived, or at St. Luke's High School, only ten minutes from our apartment. It was an easy choice; I picked the Catholic school and was thrilled with the short commute. There went my vow of never having anything to do with the church. Again.

"We need to celebrate," David said that evening when he got home.

"Where do you want to go?'

"I wasn't thinking of food. I was thinking we might go downtown to the Steinway store tomorrow morning and look around. Have you ever been there?'

I couldn't lie. "I've been there a lot. In high school, Danielle and I would take the bus downtown to go shopping every Saturday; we'd have lunch at Walgreens, and then I'd drag her to the Steinway store. Up on the eighth floor, they had the grand pianos. After a few times, the salespeople knew I could play, and they also knew I wasn't going to buy one, so they left us alone. They also knew I wasn't going to steal one."

David laughed. "Well, I guess that was one thing they never had to worry about. Shoplifting."

"I'm so excited. I wish we could go now."

"I think they're closed for the evening. Tomorrow is soon enough."

"Not for me."

I could hardly sleep that night. The next morning we drove down and when we went inside, one of the salesmen recognized me and said hello.

"Are you here to look or to buy?" he joked. He had seen me so many times.

"We're actually thinking about buying."

He smiled and got up from his desk, eager to show us everything.

"I remember you. You always played the grands, right?"

"Yes, and I know right where they are."

"I'll take you up there."

He didn't want to miss out on his commission. I understood completely and let him lead the way.

I played a few new ones, but then switched to the used grands. Their sound was just as beautiful.

"These have been completely refurbished, even though they aren't very old. New strings, hammers, and felts. This piano was made in 1952, so it isn't very old. Do you like the sound?"

"I really like it, but let me play a few more."

"I'll leave you alone for a while. See which one you like the most. I'll be back in a little while."

He left us alone and I went from one piano to the next, but it didn't take me long to realize which one I loved. It was the one I played at first, the 1952 piano. It had a deep, rich sound, and I loved it. I could imagine playing it for the rest of my life, but the price was about $8,000. I had to save enough money for rent and school, but David said, "Remember, we decided this would be our investment instead of a big wedding. Are you still okay with that?"

"Are you kidding? Of course I'm okay with it. I love it."

"Then it's yours. I'll write the check. You'll have to teach me how to play, though."

I must have gotten a frightened look on my face, because David quickly said, "Don't worry. I'm kidding. I wouldn't do that to you—or to anyone. My musical ability is in listening."

The delivery was for the next Saturday, and it was a long week of waiting. But it was worth it when I finally sat down and played all evening in our apartment. David had to tell me to stop and come to bed.

CHAPTER 4

That September, I stood in front of a classroom filled with freshman English students. It was as scary as seeing my first dead body in the basement of the motherhouse. It was actually more frightening, because there were so many students, and they were alive. And they looked at me like I was an idiot.

But I got through the first hour without acting like a complete fool. At least, I hoped so. I didn't cry and I tried to look like I knew what I was doing. I wasn't that much older than they were, and even though I hadn't been to church in a while, I made up for it with all the prayers I said as quickly as I could.

By the time I got home, I was worn out. David and I went to Steak and Shake, and afterwards I spent the entire evening frantically preparing for the next day.

He commented, "You know, they don't know nearly as much as you do. I don't think you need to prepare that much."

"I know, I know, but it makes me feel better. I need to feel in control, even though I'm not."

A week passed and I was still alive, though sometimes I questioned if I had a life outside those hours in school. It would get better; I knew it would. My mentor, Mrs. Mays, was very reassuring and supportive. And, thank God, she wasn't a nun.

I met several teachers at the school. One October afternoon, during my free period, I sat in the teacher's lounge enjoying a cup of coffee when a teacher came in and sat down across from me.

"Hi, I'm Michael. Are you new here?"

"I'm practice teaching with Mrs. Mays. Finishing up my credential."

"What's your name?"

"Kristen Byrne."

"Michael Wells." He reached out and shook my hand. He was tall, thin and black, the only black teacher I had seen at the school, although I had only been there for a few weeks and I hadn't met everyone. His hair was styled in an Afro, and he appeared young, not much older than I was.

"What do you teach?" I asked.

"Senior math classes. Calculus. Algebra 2, a few AP classes..."

"Have you been here long?"

"This is my third year. I like it here. What are you teaching? I'm guessing English?"

"Yes, mostly freshmen right now."

"So, you probably won't be staying after this semester."

"No, I'll apply to different schools in the area and see what I can get."

"How do you like it? I remember I hated practice teaching. I prefer having my own classes. It's so much easier."

"It's okay. I still feel intimidated by the students. It's scary, to be honest."

"You'll get over that. It takes time to get that confidence, especially with teenagers. Hey, what are you doing after school? Want to grab a drink at Walgreens down the street? I could give you some pointers about practice teaching, if you want."

"I'd love to." He seemed like a great person to talk to about teaching, and I felt comfortable with him already.

We drove separately to the Walgreens a block away and found a table. A few people looked at us, a white woman and a black man, but that was to be expected in St. Louis in the early 1970s. It was okay to have black friends of the same sex, but dating or the illusion of dating was still frowned upon.

We ordered drinks. I got my Dr. Pepper, and he got a Coke. We talked about school and teaching teenagers, and he shared some stories about his first few years of teaching. He didn't try to explain or teach me anything; he just shared what it had been like for him starting out, and how each semester got better as he became more comfortable with the students.

I looked at my watch and realized an hour and a half had passed.

"I'd better go. My boyfriend won't know where I am. He'll be worried."

"I'm sorry. I should have asked if you were with anyone. I hope he'll understand."

"Of course he will. I really appreciate talking to you about teaching. I hope we can do this again. It makes me feel so much better about standing up there in front of the students."

He stood and we walked out to our cars.

I thought about Michael on the way home. It was wonderful to meet a fellow teacher who was eager to discuss teaching and offer me some pointers—someone who didn't have to do it as part of their job. He was enjoyable to talk to as well. He had great stories about the kids and his teaching experiences. I could learn a lot from him.

David was home. He was cooking spaghetti and microwaving frozen meatballs.

"You're awfully late. Is everything okay? I'm usually the one who's late."

"I know. I'm sorry I didn't let you know. I met this nice teacher, and we went to Walgreens for a soda after school. He helped me a lot with my practice teaching."

"That's great. You needed some confidence building."

I told David all about Michael and how helpful he had been. David had a similar experience when he joined the police force, and he said it made all the difference in the world to have somebody who understood exactly what he was going through.

We visited some of David's friends for dinner over the weekend and had a lovely time. They were a married couple who had known him since they were all in high school together, so I got to hear every embarrassing story they could remember from those years. We laughed all evening.

They were thrilled when David told them we were engaged.

"It's about time. We didn't think it would ever happen! Congratulations. He's been waiting for you to say yes for a long time. Believe me, we've heard all about it."

David looked embarrassed, but we got onto other subjects quickly.

On the car ride home, I commented on his high-school exploits. "I'm surprised you didn't pursue the criminal side of police work instead of the actual police side."

He chuckled. "We had a great time. Most of it was quite harmless."

CHAPTER 5

One afternoon after the fifth week of school, I pulled onto the highway for the short ride home. I had plenty of room in my right lane, but a car pulled right in front of me, almost hitting me. I slammed on my brakes and hit the horn, and it moved back into its lane. Just a mistake. But the car stayed next to me, matching my speed, then pulled ahead and into my lane again. I almost ran off the road. I slowed down to let it go ahead, but it stayed with me, right next to me. It was a black car, but I couldn't identify anything else about it. Now I was scared. This was deliberate. I put on my turn signal, got off the highway at the next exit, and parked by the side of the road for a few minutes.

I didn't see the black car anymore, but I drove the rest of the way home on side streets, avoiding the highway.

Later, I told David what had happened.

"Wow, that's scary. He must have been drunk or something. Are you okay?"

"Yeah, but it was so deliberate. He didn't seem drunk. And I didn't do anything to get them angry. I mean, they were the ones who cut me off twice. I was in my own lane."

He took me in his arms. "At least you're okay. That's the important thing, that you didn't get hurt. You didn't see what kind of car it was or get a license plate?"

"No, it happened too fast, and that was the last thing I was thinking about"

"That's okay. Just some idiot. We have the whole weekend to look forward to."

"Thank God. I need it."

I lay awake that night, replaying the car incident in my mind. Some stupid driver. But why did they cut me off twice? I turned over, grateful to be next to David. He gave me such a sense of peace.

★ ★ ★

Driving into work Monday morning, I tried not to think about what had happened last week. The chances of being cut off again were infinitesimal, so I turned the radio to my favorite classical station.

I had made it through five weeks of teaching. I could do all the rest. After all, this was what I had decided to do with my life, so I'd better love it. I needed to give it some more time.

I grew more comfortable standing in front of the class, and I could see their hostility melt away slowly. Maybe it had changed to indifference, but that was okay for the moment.

I watched Mrs. Mays teach her English classes for the rest of the day, taking notes. She was a good teacher. I hoped someday to be like her, but it would take a while. I gathered up my books and got on Highway 40, heading toward the city and our apartment.

Suddenly the same black car sped up and pulled in front of me, almost hitting me again. I pulled quickly to the shoulder before I was able to get back into the lane, but it was still there. It had dropped back next to me. I tried to see what kind of car it was, but I had no idea. The windows were tinted. I slowed down, but the cars behind me were honking. And then the black car swerved in front of me again, almost hitting me. I got into the next lane, and it slowed and matched my speed. Then it got behind me. I quickly took the next exit like last time, but I didn't stop. I looked in the mirror, and it was following me. That was when I panicked. I knew not to stop by the side of the road. If there was a police station nearby, I could have pulled in there, but I saw the mall on my right and pulled into the parking lot. There were lots of cars and people. Maybe I could get the license plate. I pulled into a parking space, but it sped behind me so fast I couldn't see anything, and it drove back out on the street.

I sat in the parking lot for about ten minutes, almost in tears. What was I going to do? I had to get home. I pulled out onto the road parallel to the highway and drove home on surface streets again, watching every car behind me or at my side with a sense of panic.

I got home without any more problems, but I went inside, sat on the couch, and cried. JC and Alex curled up beside me, wondering what was wrong, but I couldn't even pet them.

David walked in the door and called, "How was your day?"

I couldn't answer him. He came around to the front of the couch and saw I'd been crying. He sat down and took my hands.

"It'll get better. I know you'll be a great teacher."

"No, it's not that. I nearly got run off the road again by the same car. It followed me into the mall parking lot and sped away."

"What? Tell me exactly what happened."

I told him everything.

He looked angrier and angrier as I told him.

"I can't let anything else happen to you. Can you think of anyone, anyone at all, who might want to hurt you?"

I shook my head. "I don't know. We've been involved in so many investigations. There could be a lot of people, but most of them are in jail."

"Hey, tomorrow I'm going to follow you to work and be right behind you when you come home. Maybe I can see what kind of car it is and who's driving it—and get the license number. At least I'll be there, watching out for you."

I nodded my head, so grateful that he was going to do that. I was really scared. One time was upsetting, but twice wasn't a coincidence. Someone was out there to scare me, or hurt me, or both. But I wasn't involved in any investigation right now. All those were in the past, and everyone who had committed the murders was in jail.

"Let's have something for dinner," he said.

"Okay. I haven't fixed anything."

"That's okay. How about our favorite Italian?"

"Okay." I didn't really feel like eating, but it was probably what I needed.

David fed the cats so they wouldn't starve, and we headed out for dinner.

CHAPTER 6

As we sat in the crowded restaurant, David pulled out his small notebook from his shirt pocket, set it on the table, and turned to a blank page.

"I know you don't want to think about this now, but we have to. Let's start from the beginning. The very first investigation I was involved in, Joan and Maribeth and the chalice. Was there anyone else involved? Anyone who might have been angry about Maribeth or the role that Inez played in the investigation?"

I sat there, twirling my pasta absentmindedly on my fork.

"Maribeth and Inez were the only ones ever involved in that. I can't think of anyone else who might have been upset or offended by anything I did."

"Maribeth's in jail, but that doesn't mean she couldn't arrange for someone to threaten you and harass you."

"But she knew very few people here in the St. Louis area. She's from Mankato, Minnesota, where we have our northern province."

"She could have met someone in jail. You have no idea who she knows."

"Well, that's true."

"So, we can't rule her out." David moved on to the next murder investigation. "Well, the sisters in Franklin dislike both of us. The superior there, Sister Janine, isn't very happy with the two of us, along with her relatives. And Sister Hilda doesn't think very highly of us since Sister Martha got in trouble."

"But Sister Hilda's so old. She's not going to come into the city and try to cut me off on the highway."

"No, but she might know someone who would do it for her. That's the problem. Or she might be helping out Sister Martha."

"Sister Inez hates me."

"Is she still in the area?"

"I heard from someone, probably Linda, that she got a job through one of her former students selling commercial real estate in north St. Louis."

"Okay, so she's still on the list, and don't forget Sister Jeanette, who wrote those horrible letters to Patricia and Linda."

"I guess I never realized I have so many people who hate me."

David put down his fork, reached across the table, and took my hand.

"They all hate me too. But remember, they were people who did bad things and deserved punishment. It's not your fault. You're not hated by innocent, kind people. But we still need to figure out who's behind this. I don't want you to live in fear all the time."

"I know. I can't go on like this. It's horrible, but how will we figure out who's doing it?"

"They'll make a mistake. They always do. I hope it happens soon, for your sake. Let's complete the list."

"There are so many terrible people."

"But don't forget all the good people we've met in the past few years. Your friend Sister Joan, Pam, many of your classmates, Sister Jeanette's brother, who became a lawyer, Sister Anne, the housekeeper at the parish, the two priests at St. Boniface, your priest friend from the convent, Father Stephen. The list is long."

"I guess you're right. I can't concentrate on the bad people. There are so many wonderful people I know."

"We *will* solve this. And I promise nothing will happen to you."

"You can't promise that." I was almost in tears.

"I know, but I can try as hard as possible."

"I'm so lucky I met you."

"I'm not so sure about that. You probably wouldn't have gotten involved in all these investigations."

"Yeah, maybe it wasn't worth it." But I didn't mean that at all.

"Hey, don't go that far." He leaned over and kissed me.

"Okay, okay, it was worth it. What do we do next?" I asked.

"Well, I can't really interview any of these people. That would probably be useless. We have no evidence against anyone, only guesses as to who might have a grudge against you and me. I can't ask questions randomly. But I would like to find out where everyone is living and what they've been doing since they've left the convent or gotten out of jail."

I was reluctant to even suggest this. "I'm sure there are a lot of people at the motherhouse who know where everyone is. I could ask people like Linda or Sister Miriam John what everyone is doing."

"No, sorry. You can't be involved in any of this. I can find out where everyone is. I don't want you involved at all. Just knowing what we've talked about tonight gives me leads about where to concentrate."

"I hope you can find something out soon."

"And I can tell you where they all are and what they're doing. It's not exactly classified information. I'll tell you when I find out something interesting. I'm going to call Vincent Marino in the morning. He'll be able to tell me about Sister Jeanette, his sister, and I trust that he'll give me reliable information about her. She's on the short list."

★ ★ ★

David called the law offices the following morning, but Mr. Marino was in court for the day, so David asked to have his call returned as soon as possible. He received a call back about 4 p.m. that afternoon from Marino.

"This is Sheriff David Kelly, the detective who was working on the murder case of Sister Patricia."

"Yes, I remember, of course."

"I'm calling about your sister, Sister Jeanette. Is she still in the convent? Do you feel comfortable sharing that information with me?"

"Why? Is there a problem? I know Jeanette served her time for sending those letters to Sister Patricia. And you know she's not a sister anymore?"

"Yes, I realize that. Kristen, my fiancée, has been the subject of some threats recently, and I wanted to rule out Jeanette right away. You don't have to share any information with me, as you know."

"Well, I'm sorry to hear that, but I'm afraid I won't be much help, and you don't need to bring me in to question me. After Jeanette got released from jail, I gave her some money—actually, it was ten thousand dollars, because she had nothing at all—and that was the last contact we had. It was about a year ago. She had left the convent before she served her time, and I have no idea where she is now. And frankly, I have no desire to be in touch with her. I told her that last year. The fact that she used me for her little scheme without my knowledge or consent was unforgivable."

"I'm sorry that's how your relationship ended, but it sounds like it's for the best. I appreciate you giving me this information. You've always been very cooperative."

"I wish I could do more to help. Good luck with finding out about those threats."

"Thank you."

David hoped he'd find Jeanette some other way. He wouldn't want to have anything to do with her either, even if she was family. Sometimes relationships turned so toxic that you had to let them go. He knew that from experience.

He concentrated on finding the other people on their list. He got Linda's phone number from Kristen and called her. She was happy to hear from him since she clearly felt they had become friends during the time she had stayed with Kristen during the last investigation. She said she was thrilled to know they were back together.

"I knew it would work out, David. She loves you so much."

"Thank you." David was embarrassed. "What's happening with you, Linda? I see you're living in Wentzville. Isn't that where your parents live?"

"Yeah, I'm trying to finish up my teaching credential, but I had to put it on hold because my dad is sick. He has cancer, and my mom can't take care of him, so I'm at home helping them. I don't think he's going to live for much longer, probably no more than six months."

"I'm sorry to hear that. It's so good of you to be there helping them. There's nobody like family at a time like this."

"I'm glad I'm able to do it."

David told her what was happening to Kristen and asked if she knew where some of the people were.

"Well, everybody knows about Inez. She got kicked out, or asked to leave, as soon as she went to jail, and when she got out, she moved up to Chicago. She couldn't get a teaching job because of the conviction, but she moved back here and is working at a real estate company, selling commercial property. I imagine she'd be good at that."

"Do you know anything about Sister Jeanette? Where she might be?"

"Well, she left the convent too, because of all the hate mail to Pat and me. I think she's still in the St. Louis area, but the only person she's kept in touch with is Sister Karin, the head of the junior sisters. Why they kept in touch, I don't know, but that's what I heard."

"Linda, you've been a big help. I wish you the best with your father. What kind of cancer does he have?"

"He has lung cancer. He smoked heavily his whole life, and I'm sure that didn't help. They can't do anything at this point."

"I'm sorry. You take care and stay in touch. Let us know how you are."

"I will. I promise."

David hung up the phone, saddened by the information about her father but knowing he had gotten a few leads. As he thought more about it, though, he realized he hadn't really gotten anything at all. All these people had family, and even if they weren't driving the car that threatened Kristen, they could have asked anyone in their family or acquaintances to do it for them.

Linda didn't know anything about people in Franklin. He'd have to find out about them from other sources. And no one seemed to know the whereabouts of Jeanette. Well, someone would, but it certainly wouldn't be Linda, one of Jeanette's hate-mail recipients.

David was tired and was glad to get home. Kristen had fixed some mac and cheese and a salad.

"I'm not a great cook, as you know, probably somewhere between our Italian restaurant and Steak and Shake. Closer to Steak and Shake."

David sat down with the two cats trying to get on his lap. "It's perfect. I couldn't ask for anything better."

"Good, because we'd have to pay for something better."

"I'm happy staying here."

He told her about the conversation with Linda.

"I'm so sorry about her dad. And what's her mom going to do?"

"I didn't ask about her mom. I wonder if she'll be able to take care of herself when her husband dies. She might have to go into a home up there in Wentzville."

"I need to call her. I feel bad I haven't kept in touch. I meant to."

*

I called Linda the next evening and had a long talk with her after apologizing for not calling sooner. David wasn't great at getting the convent gossip, but I learned as much as I could. Since Linda was out of the convent, she didn't know much more than I did, but she filled me in on Sister Inez and a few other people at the motherhouse. I understood what a difficult year Linda had without Patricia, but I hadn't realized she was still suffering so deeply. She was in tears for most of the conversation, and she told me that the worst part was not having anyone to confide in about her love for Patricia. She couldn't tell her parents, especially now that her father was so ill. She carried all this grief inside her with nowhere for it to go. We talked for a long time.

David followed me into work for the next week, then came by the school after class and followed my car home afterwards. There were no more incidents, and I started to relax a little.

Michael saw me in the teacher's lounge and asked if I'd like to go get a soda with him again the next week. I asked him to come outside with me so we could talk privately. We sat on one of the benches by the football field.

"So why did we need to come out here? I only asked if you wanted to get some coffee or soda."

"Well, it's complicated."

"It seems pretty simple to me." Then he looked down at the ground. "Does your boyfriend object to us being together? We're just friends—or is it because I'm Black? Is that the problem? Don't worry. This isn't the first time it's happened."

I felt terrible that he would think that, although I realized my family was very liberal about civil rights, more so than most people we knew.

"No, not at all. And David was so happy I had someone to talk to about teaching. I have this other problem, though, and I wanted to tell you privately because I don't want anyone else to know about it." I told him about the person who had tried to run me off the road and how David was following me to school and back home every afternoon.

"Wow, that's frightening. Why do you think someone would do that? Does someone have something against you?"

I had to tell him about all the murder investigations I had been involved with in the last few years. Michael listened quietly, but I could see he was shocked that this young, quiet teacher could have such a colorful past already, and I wasn't even twenty-three years old.

I finished my story.

He looked up at me. "I had no idea you were involved in so many investigations—and so many murders! You look so, well, normal, I guess. I can't believe someone wants to hurt you."

"You might not want to stay around me too long," I joked. "Although I try to keep my distance from nuns and priests."

"Well, you're not doing a very good job of it, teaching in a Catholic school."

"I know, I know. It was the closest school, though, and I couldn't see driving for almost an hour when this school was only ten minutes away."

"Well, I'm not a nun or a priest, so I'm probably pretty safe." He laughed, and then stopped laughing quickly, realizing he was talking about murders.

He glanced at his watch, probably thinking of his next class. "Where do you live?"

I told him. He said quickly, "That's on my way home. I could follow you home and take over your boyfriend's job a few days a week if you want. I don't know if I'd be as good as he is, but I probably could get a license plate number if I tried, especially if they weren't trying to push me off the road. And I could figure out the make and model of the car. I know cars pretty well."

"That's so nice of you to offer. It's not easy for David to take me and come and get me every day, but he insists on it."

"Well, ask him. Then we could have coffee and talk whenever we wanted."

I wasn't sure what David would think about my friendship with Michael either. So far it was strictly professional, but I could sense Michael was interested in me. And I thought he was a wonderful, kind person whom I loved having as a friend. I worried that maybe I liked him a little too much. No, I loved David. I was sure of that. I was so inexperienced, I didn't know how to deal with my feelings. When would I ever learn? I hoped it would be soon. I decided to ask David very soon about what Michael had offered.

CHAPTER 7

I had been polite to all the nuns teaching at the school, but tried to keep my distance. I was very glad that my mentor, Mrs. Mays, was a lay teacher, married with three children. I didn't need to be friends with any more nuns or priests.

I took a deep breath one morning when, sitting in the teacher's lounge, Sister Mary Patrick came in and sat down across from me. She seemed only a few years older than I was, and she looked like she wanted to talk.

"Can I ask you a question?" She was direct. No small talk for her.

"Sure," I answered, hoping it would be a simple question about my teaching schedule or something related to it.

"You got your degree at Washington University in English, right?"

That was simple. "Yes. This past year."

"And you were in the convent for a short time. Notre Dame? Right?"

"Yes, that's right. I wasn't even in for a whole year."

"Well, I've been writing a book, and I'm wondering if you would mind reading through it and telling me what you think. It's a book about meditation. I was thinking with your English degree and your religious background, you might be the perfect person to give me your opinion."

"I'm not very religious anymore." I wanted to clear that up right away.

"That's okay. In fact, it's even better. It's meditation techniques for everyone, not just for religious people. And I'd really appreciate your input."

"I'm not sure I'm the right person, but I'd be glad to read it."

"Thank you. I'll bring it in tomorrow."

She got up quickly and walked out of the room.

Great. Just what I didn't want to do: read a book about meditation. When I was a postulant—a first-year student—we had to get up at four thirty, be in the chapel by five, and meditate for an hour before Mass every morning. As you can imagine, a lot of our meditation was merely a continuation of our sleep from the previous night. We never received any lectures or lessons on how to meditate; we were expected to sit there and figure it out ourselves, which I never did. Oh, I thought about many things, but I didn't believe it was meditation.

Maybe I'd learn something from her book. Not that I'd ever use it. Why I said I'd read it, I didn't know. I was merely trying to be polite.

When I saw David in the parking lot that afternoon and he followed me home without any incident, I had a lot to tell him. He was very sure that Michael shouldn't follow me in the afternoons.

"That's police work, and if anything happened to him because I had agreed to let him help with an investigation, it would be my fault. I could never risk that. And I'm fine with following you until we're sure the threat is over. "

It had been quiet for about a week, and I was hopeful that the harassment had ended.

* * *

I pulled out Sister Mary Patrick's manuscript later that night. I had finished all my preparations for the next day—for the next week—and even though reading about meditation was the last thing I wanted to do, I also wanted to get it over with. I went into the spare bedroom where I kept my briefcase, took out the manuscript, sat down, and started to read.

Meditation is for everyone, not just for religious people. It is an art which can be learned and practiced and is of great benefit...

I knew the book was going to be boring, but a promise was a promise. I turned the page and kept reading.

She stared at him and suddenly his lips were on hers, his hands on her breasts, her heart beating fast. He pushed her down on the bed, and she—

This wasn't about meditation! I looked at the first page again, then the second page. I kept reading. I thought at first she had made a mistake, that she accidentally put another manuscript page in the meditation book, even though that seemed very odd. But the wild, erotic encounter went on and on. I couldn't put it down. They were really going at it. And her descriptions were very graphic.

David came into the bedroom. "Are you going to bed? It's almost eleven. That meditation book must be fascinating," he said with a laugh.

I closed the manuscript quickly, as if I were a guilty child and had just been caught.

"You can keep reading. I wanted to let you know I'm going to bed."

"No, I am too. I mean, yes, I'm tired. Let's go to bed."

I smiled to myself as I brushed my teeth. I could hardly wait to tell David, but I could wait until morning. And I could hardly wait to talk to Sister Mary Patrick about this "meditation book."

★ ★ ★

The next morning, we were sitting at the dining room table. David was drinking his coffee and reading the *St. Louis Post-Dispatch.*

"I have to tell you something."

He put down the paper. "Sure. I was just reading the comics."

"You know that book on meditation?"

"That one you were so interested in last night?"

"Yes. Well, it isn't about meditation."

"What do you mean?"

"The first page is, and then it turns into a sexy romance novel. I couldn't believe it. I mean, she really goes into detail."

"So that's why you couldn't put it down." He laughed.

"Well, maybe. And I did promise her that I would read it."

"Yeah, right. Can I read it too?"

"Maybe we should read it together?"

"You think I need some new ideas?"

I blushed, like I always did. "No, I think you have plenty of ideas. But it would be fun."

He laughed again, then stopped quickly. "What's a nun doing writing a book like that and giving it to you to read? I don't get it. What's the point?"

"I don't get it either. I can hardly wait to ask her. I guess she can't show it to anyone else and figured I would be the best person since I got kicked out? I don't know. I can't figure it out. She told me I have the only other manuscript besides hers."

"That's weird. You need to talk to her. She doesn't even know you that well, right?"

"Right. She's only talked to me a few times in the teacher's lounge. That's it. I've really been trying to avoid the priests and nuns at the school."

We got ready to head to school. David was going to follow me again.

"It's been over three weeks. I hate for you to keep doing this."

David didn't even bother to answer. He got in his car and followed me onto the highway. I said goodbye to him in the school parking lot and he was there at 3 p.m. when I walked back out to the lot. I was glad to see him. We drove down Highway 40 and suddenly the black car was next to me. I swerved and almost hit another car as I went onto the shoulder before I swerved back into my lane. The car dropped back and then did the same maneuver a second time. I slowed down as the black car sped ahead and I could see David's car behind it. I got off at the next exit, pulled to the side of the road, and waited. David would come back.

I hoped he wouldn't get hurt or confront the driver, but I prayed this would settle the matter for good. I waited and waited. I was ready to start the car and go home when David pulled up.

"He's gone. I'll follow you home. You'll be fine."

I started the car and drove home with David behind me in his.

When we were in his apartment, I collapsed on the couch. The kitties came running to see us.

David came into the living room and sat next to me. "I got his license plate, and I'll run it tomorrow. I hope we can solve this soon. I know things have been really rough for you lately, but they'll get better. I promise. And I'm sure our talk a few nights ago didn't help either."

I nodded between the tears. "I want to get married and be with you. I hope the difference about children doesn't mean we can't be together."

I kept crying.

David pushed me away from him. "Look at me. No, I mean it. Look at me. Nothing, I mean nothing, is going to come between us. We're going to have disagreements and arguments, and this is something we're going to have to talk about. But nothing is going to make me love you less. I promise you that."

"Have you ever been in love before?" I managed to ask him.

He took a while to answer. "I want to say no, but I have to be honest with you. There was someone I really loved a few years ago. We were engaged and I was ready to spend my life with her. I thought she felt the same about me. But she seemed to get more distant as the months went by, and one night she finally told me she had fallen in love with someone else and wanted to break off the engagement. In fact, she wanted to break off everything and never communicate again. She packed up all her things and left the next morning. That was the last time I ever spoke to her. It was incredibly hard to let her go, but I didn't have a choice. I heard she got pregnant and had a child, and got divorced a few years later. I don't know what happened to her after that."

"Do you ever want to see her or talk to her?"

"No, it would be like opening a wound and making it bleed all over again. I couldn't do that. Besides, meeting you helped me forget about her. I have no desire to go back, now that I have you."

CHAPTER 8

"We should get going," David said the following day. "I'm still going to follow you until I hear about that license plate. I hope I hear today. It's been two days. They should be getting back to me today, or tomorrow at the latest. It takes a while. I had to call the numbers into the DMV, and they had to start the process of looking up the plates. There are thousands of plates, but we should have the information soon. I think the person was aware I was following them, so maybe that'll put a stop to it. I'll still follow you, though, until we know."

I grabbed everything I needed for school, and we headed out. I hoped I would see Michael today. I really enjoyed talking to him, especially about his teaching experience. He was full of stories, not only about teaching, but about a life that was so different than mine. It was fascinating. I liked that we were becoming friends. I worried a little that I liked him, but it was purely a professional arrangement. If it weren't for David, perhaps it could have been more.

I arrived at Sister Mary Patrick's homeroom before the first bell and walked in as the students were taking their seats and talking. "I need to talk to you."

"Did you read the book?"

"Yes, are you free seventh period?"

"Yes, I'll meet you in the teacher's lounge."

"Okay, I'll see you there."

I couldn't help thinking about the book all day. I could hardly wait until seventh period. When I came in and sat down, she was already at the table with a cup of coffee. A few other teachers were also there.

"I have those papers in my homeroom," she said simply.

"Okay." We both got up, and I followed her down the corridor to her empty classroom. There were a few students at their lockers, getting out books, but when they saw us, they closed their lockers and moved quickly down the hall.

We got to her classroom and sat in two students' chairs in front.

"I don't understand," I started simply.

"You don't really think that a book on meditation would sell? I want to publish this, make some money, and get out of here."

"Out of this school, or out of the convent?"

"Do you think I would stay in the convent after writing a book like that?"

"Well, no."

"How did you like it? I was taking a big chance by having you read it."

"I couldn't put it down," I answered honestly.

She smiled broadly. "I knew I picked the right person."

"And I think it will sell. But how are you going to get it published? Are you going to use another name?"

"I don't know yet. So far, you're the only person I've shown it to. I have my copy and I made a copy here at school for you, but that's it. I don't want anybody else to know. I guess I'll try to publish it under a pen name if I can find a publisher, maybe get some money—and then leave. And I'm not naïve—people don't make a living off writing books—but I think I'll make more than I would from a book about meditation."

"Do you have a pen name picked out?"

"No, not yet. Maybe you can help me with that?"

"Me? I have no idea."

We talked about a lot of silly pen names that she could choose, Candy and Diamond and Tiffany. She liked Tiffany.

"What about a last name?" she asked.

"I don't know."

"How about a color, like orange, or purple, or blue? I kind of like blue."

"Tiffany Blue. That sounds good."

"Not that I'll ever use it," she said.

"Hey, don't say that. I think it's a great book. I think you'll get it published. I'm going to see it in a bookstore someday soon."

"I hope so."

"And I'm happy it wasn't about meditating. I was dreading the thought of reading about meditating. Sorry."

"Don't be sorry."

"You must have had a lot of experience before you went into the convent. At least, more than I did."

"Experience with meditating, or with sex?"

I laughed. "Well, I didn't mean meditating. I didn't have experience with either one."

She got serious. "I hope none of it offended you."

"No, it just surprised me. Can I share some of it with my boyfriend?"

"Only if you promise that it's only the two of you that will be reading it."

"I promise."

"I did have some experience. And I don't really know why I went into the convent. I was angry at my last boyfriend after we broke up. That's the very worst reason to become a nun, but I did it anyway. Sometimes I can be impulsive, as you might have gathered by now."

"Yeah, I think I got that."

"Thanks for reading it. You can keep the copy, but please don't share it with anyone."

"It's safe with me. Don't worry. I'll never show it to anyone except David."

★ ★ ★

David got the information about the license plates that day, but it wasn't very helpful. They were traced to a car-rental company, and the company looked up who the car had been rented to when I had been followed, but it wasn't what David had hoped for. The car had been rented to a security company in St. Louis: Winston Security. It was a large security company that guarded many of the office buildings in the city and county. Now he had to trace who'd had that particular car on those weeks or days, but it could have been any number of drivers who worked for the company.

"Don't worry. I'm not going to give up," David assured me. "It would have been easier if it had been an individual who owned the car, but I'll just have to work a little harder."

"I have something to tell you too, about the manuscript that Sister Mary Patrick gave me a few weeks ago. I talked to her today."

"This should be interesting. Tell me." We sat on the couch, petting the cats, as usual. There was nothing on TV, so we had a lot of time to talk about our day.

"She wants to leave as soon as she can. She went into the convent because of a relationship that didn't work out, and now she really regrets going in, but she doesn't have enough money to leave. She only has a mom and a sister, and they don't talk to each other. So she wants to publish this book and make some money, then leave."

"It's hard to make money publishing books, isn't it?"

"Well, she'll probably make a lot more from her romance book than a book on meditation."

David laughed. "That's for sure. I can't even think of anyone who would read a book about meditation, although I hear it's getting a lot more popular these days for relieving stress. And God knows we need something for that. It has to be better than taking pills."

"I asked her if she had a pen name, but she didn't yet, so we came up with one together. I wonder if she'll use it. And, oh, she said you could read it too."

"Do you think I need some advice?"

I blushed, as usual.

"No, of course not. It's something we can laugh at together, I hope."

"Okay, now I want to read it. I'm not sure I've ever read anything quite like it. I mean, *Playboy* probably isn't quite like that. The articles are very scientific. That's what everyone says who buys it. I wouldn't know, of course. Maybe I can get some tips from this book."

I laughed. "I hope not!"

"Do you think you'll keep in touch with her after practice teaching?"

"She seems like a good person. I think I'd like to, and she doesn't really count as a nun since she's going to be leaving her order."

David smiled. "You always know how to get around the boundaries you've set for yourself. I thought you said no more nuns or priests forever."

"Well, I did say that, and I meant it, but she's leaving, so she doesn't really count as a nun."

"That's why I love you. You can weasel out of anything, can't you?"

He leaned over and gave me a long kiss, so I didn't bother answering him.

★ ★ ★

CHAPTER 9

David couldn't interview all the people we suspected of trying to run into me, especially now that he'd learned the car had been rented by a security agency instead of a person.

"I'm going to have to find out all the organizations in St. Louis that use this particular security company and see if I can make any connections between them and anyone on our list. I don't know what else I can do. I can't call the sisters into the station without evidence and ask if they've been following you and trying to run you off the road. I need something more substantial."

"How are you ever going to find anything?"

"I don't know, but I will. I'm not going to let anything happen to you."

* * *

I told David that I'd like to be able to talk to Michael more often without worrying about David's schedule, because he still insisted on following me.

"Just let me know when you're going someplace to talk, then go to a telephone booth and call the station when you're ready to leave. It'll give me more time at work, which will be a good thing. I've been leaving a little too early most days to follow you home. I have a lot of work to catch up on."

I told Michael the next day and he was fine with that. We made plans for the following day and met after school. He had a large family and always had new stories about his nephews, nieces, and cousins that were delightful to hear. And I could tell him anything about my teaching, and he encouraged me and assured me it would be better in time.

I could also tell him about my life and all the investigations I had been involved with. He was fascinated with my stories; he had never experienced anything like that in his life. We could easily talk for hours. I called David and he met me in the parking lot of Walgreens to follow me home. He met Michael and seemed to like him, even during their brief encounters. There wasn't much chance of me being followed because I was going home at such random times. And I'd be finished with my practice-teaching in less than a week, so I hoped all the threats would be over permanently.

We were tired and went to bed earlier than usual. I woke up at three o'clock with the sound of the phone ringing in the dining room. David got up to answer it. That was the line the police had for his regular and emergency number in case they needed to reach him. It was his only number, and I was using David's number. I had given it to only a few people, my parents, Pam, and a few friends at school. He came back in a minute and climbed back into bed.

"Who was it?" I asked sleepily.

"Nobody. A wrong number, I guess. They hung up."

I must have fallen back asleep quickly, but I heard the phone ring again. David got up to answer it a second time. He came back and slipped into bed. "Same thing. No answer."

I could tell he was annoyed. I was too. It was harder to fall back asleep this time. I lay awake until it started to get light. David breathed gently beside me; at least, he was sleeping. I was glad, because he needed to rest for his job, more than I did.

We stayed in bed until after seven the next morning because it was Saturday. I got dressed and drove to the doughnut shop down the street, where I bought four old-fashioned doughnuts for us—our usual Saturday-morning treat.

"What was that all about last night?" I asked as I munched on the donut and drank hot chocolate.

"I don't know, but it was sure annoying. I hope it doesn't happen again."

"Me too."

But it did happen again. On Saturday night, we got three phone calls with hang-ups, and I finally offered to answer the next one that night, but it didn't ring again. We were both in cranky moods all day Sunday, hoping the calls wouldn't happen the next night. David hesitated to take the phone off the hook because if there was an emergency, he had to be available and this was the line they would call.

We went to sleep early that night. At 3 a.m., like clockwork, the phone rang again.

"Don't get it," I whispered.

"I have to." He got out of bed, but it was the same thing. The person hung up immediately, calling back each hour until the morning.

"Okay, I'm going to get a new number for me, and we'll leave that old one off the hook at night. Is that okay with you?"

"Yes, at least until you can trace the number. You can do that, can't you?"

"Yes, but it'll take a few days. It's complicated, but the switchboard at the AT&T phone center can do that with the records they have from the last few nights."

"Do you think it's connected to the other threats I've been getting?"

"Yes, I do. I don't know what else it could be. But I don't know why they're using my number."

"Maybe because I don't have my own number anymore."

"If we can find out who's making these calls, we might find out who's responsible for both. I sure hope so, anyway."

★ ★ ★

Monday was difficult. I was exhausted and could hardly think straight. Mrs. Mays noticed my fatigue right away.

"Do you want me to teach today.? You look terrible. Are you sure you're okay?"

"If you don't mind teaching, that would be great." She was so nice.

"We only have a week left before the semester is over. I think you've done a great job. I could give you your grades now and even let you take the rest of the time off if you need to?"

"No, I'm sure I'll be okay. My fiancé and I have been getting some crank calls in the middle of the night, and that's been keeping us up for about a week, but I think that'll be over very soon."

"That's terrible. Why do you think it'll be over soon?"

"He's a policeman, and he can trace the calls, so we should be able to find out soon who's making them."

I had never told her about the other threats involving my car, so this was the first clue she had that anything was wrong. I wanted it that way. I wanted to finish my practice teaching like a normal person, without any special requests for time off.

CHAPTER 10

When I came home that day, a telephone company employee was at our apartment installing a new line. I was so glad for David and for me. We could turn off his phone at night, and he'd have the new one for the department to call in an emergency.

He got a new phone for me too. "You need one that's separate from mine."

I'd let my parents know my new number and I hoped that would put an end to the annoying phone calls. We'd finally be able to sleep, I hoped. He didn't yet know where the calls had originated, though. That would take a few more days.

We decided to go out for dinner. It had been a while since we had been to our favorite Italian place, and we decided it was time to celebrate something—anything, actually. A new phone number was enough.

He took a little box from his pocket as I was eating cheesecake, and pushed it over to me.

"I don't know if you'll like this, but I wanted to at least see if you want it. It was my grandmother's, and my father took it back from my mother when they got divorced. It was in his things when he died, and he wanted me to give it to the person I married, if I ever got married. You don't have to wear it, though. Only if you like it."

I slowly opened the box. It was a beautiful fire opal ring. He reached over and put it on my finger. "It's not a diamond, and if you want a diamond, I can get you a diamond engagement ring, but I've always loved this ring."

"David, I love it. I really do. I love opals, and I don't care about diamonds. This is much more beautiful, and it's special to you because of your grandmother and father. It's special to me because you love it. I love you."

"I'm so glad. Now I don't have to get one."

I stared at him. He laughed. "You know I'm only joking."

"I ought to know by now." And I should have. He had a wonderful sense of humor, which I appreciated, especially since it had been such a hard week and month. I needed some fun in my life.

CHAPTER 11

David came home the next afternoon with some news. We sat down at the dining room table.

"They were able to trace the calls. But unfortunately, they all came from a telephone booth on Grand Avenue. I don't have a name or an address to check out. I'll go down there tomorrow or when I have time and see what's around the area—see if there's anything familiar that I recognize. But I kind of doubt it. And even if it was someone who worked in one of the buildings around the area, if there are any, what would they be doing there at night? It's all very confusing. But I'll see if I can get some answers tomorrow. I have another big case I'm working on, so I don't have much time. It's a fraud case regarding the banking industry and it's pretty complex, so I've been spending a lot of time on that. I'll try to find time tomorrow, though."

"A telephone booth? That's strange. Who would be hanging out for hours at a time at a telephone booth? For so many nights in a row? I'm anxious to see what you can find out."

"Yeah, me too."

★ ★ ★

David checked out the area with the telephone booth. There was nothing obvious. Large office buildings surrounded it. He glanced at the tenant names in the buildings, but nothing stood out as significant. A clothing manufacturer's headquarters, an aviation company that built Cessnas, a few corporate law firms, accounting firms, a State Farm representative, and a dentist—nothing out of the ordinary.

He went to all the buildings on the block, but couldn't imagine anyone working in any of those firms staying around until three in the morning to make phone calls. He decided to call the security firm that protected the offices. It was the same security company that had rented the car that had followed Kristen.

"Winston Security."

"This is Sergeant David Kelly from the St. Louis Police Department."

"Oh, how can I help you?"

"I need to come down to speak with your boss today or tomorrow about a car rental that was made in your firm's name."

"Was there a problem with the car, sir?"

"No, I just need to get some information about how you use rental cars for your business."

"Mr. Philips is available tomorrow morning. I can put you down anytime then, sir."

"I'll be there around nine. If you could please tell him I'm coming to get some information, I'd appreciate that."

"Of course. I'll let him know."

★ ★ ★

David was at Winston Security in the morning. Mr. Philips asked him to come into his office, where they both sat down.

"I'm investigating the license number of a car that was rented to your security company for the past three weeks."

"Why? Has something happened to the car?"

"The driver of the car has been accused of dangerous driving and trying to run someone off the freeway at least three times. I was following him the last time and got his license number. I found out it was rented to your company."

"That's awful. Let me look up who was driving the car, if you give me the dates and times."

David gave him the dates, and he went to the secretary and asked her to look up the information in the files.

She brought the information to them in less than five minutes and Mr. Philips looked over the ledger carefully.

"Arthur Schmidt. He got fired last week. We found out he had three speeding tickets in the past two months in his own vehicle. We can't have anybody like that working for us. He's young; when he got hired, he was squeaky clean, but I don't know what happened to him. Anyway, he's gone."

"I'll need his home number and address."

"I'll write them down for you. I'm sorry an employee of ours was so much trouble, but you can be sure it won't happen again."

"Why do you rent cars for your employees?"

"We don't do it often, but sometimes our cars are in for repairs and we have to rent one. That's the car rental place we usually use. They're very reliable."

David got up to leave. "Thanks for your help. I appreciate it."

"Of course. I hope you can find him and discover what happened."

Mr. Philips walked David out to the front door. David's next stop was Arthur Schmidt's address. It was in Florissant, about a half-hour drive. David hoped he could catch him at home. If all went well, this would be the end of the harassment. Kristen didn't need the worry. She had so much to worry about, with her teaching, their phone calls in the middle of the night, and all the murder investigations, which didn't ever seem to be over.

He arrived at a small brick home on a quiet street off Patterson Road. He parked in front of the house for a few minutes. No cars were on the street, and none were in the carport. The lawn was well manicured, and the flower beds were in full bloom.

He rang the doorbell and waited a few minutes. Someone called, "Who is it?" to which he replied, "St. Louis Police."

A grey-haired lady opened the door cautiously and regarded him for a moment, as if she didn't believe him. He held up his badge since he wasn't wearing his uniform.

"What do you want?"

"Does Arthur Schmidt live here? I'd like to speak with him."

"Yes, he does, sometimes, but he's not here right now. He's at work."

"Where does he work?"

She looked confused. "I don't remember. He got his new job a few days ago. It's in a bakery or something like that."

"Did he give you a telephone number where he can be reached?"

"No," was her abrupt answer.

She was not helping at all.

"Are you his mother?"

"Yes, I am. What has he done?'

"I need to talk to him about that, ma'am."

"He used to get in a lot of trouble, but he's a lot better now. He has a job and he's living here with us and paying rent and everything."

"When are you expecting him home from work?"

"Not for a while."

David was getting frustrated with her lack of help. "Ma'am, I need to speak with him. You need to cooperate with me and let me know how to reach him, or I'll have to wait here until he comes back."

She relented. "Let me go in his room and see if I can find out where he's working. Maybe it's in there somewhere."

She walked away from the door and left David standing outside. That was fine. He didn't want to go inside. All he wanted was to talk to the man. He might even be inside, but David didn't have a search warrant.

A few minutes later, she came back to the door. "I was wrong. It's an auto parts shop. It's about a block away. Hayes Auto. If you go back down the street and turn left, you should see it on the right."

"Thank you, ma'am." He turned and walked back to his car. Of course, she'd known where he was working the whole time. It was probably owned by his father or cousin, and they were letting him work there until he got fired again. There wasn't any point in arguing with her, though.

He drove down the street and turned left, spotting a few shops by the side of the road. One was Hayes Auto. He pulled up in front, next to some cars that were being worked on.

He walked inside and addressed the receptionist, a young Italian girl who was quite beautiful but clearly bored with her job, as she inspected her nails carefully.

"I'd like to speak to Arthur Schmidt, please."

She finally looked up at him.

"I'm a police officer from the St. Louis Police Department." He showed her his badge.

She was paying close attention to him now.

"There's no one here by that name, sir."

"Are you sure?"

"Yes, sir, I know all the employees by name. I fill out the payroll and work schedules, so I know."

A person at the next counter asked her, "Isn't he a friend of George's? He comes in every week or so, and they go out for lunch."

"I don't know." She kept looking at David, eyeing him with interest.

"Can you ask George?" he asked her.

"Okay, I'll call him from the back. Thanks, Eddie."

She turned from the counter and walked through the door to the back of the store.

She came back out with George, who was wiping the grease off his hands with a red cloth.

"Can I help you, officer?"

"Do you know Arthur Schmidt?"

"Yeah, he comes in here to pick up money that someone leaves for him. We usually go out and pick up lunch. I knew him from high school. I don't think he's doing anything right now except living with his mother. He's been in a lot of trouble."

"Where does he get the money?"

"He never told me that. A man comes in and leaves an envelope with me, addressed to Arthur, and I give it to him when he comes in. I don't ask any questions. I just give it to him."

"Do you have an envelope for him now?"

"No, the guy hasn't come in for a while."

Okay, thanks for your time. I appreciate it."

David walked back to his car. He didn't think the people in the auto shop were lying. Arthur was being paid by someone to harass Kristen, and probably to call them on the phone at all hours of the night. He was getting paid for a job, not even knowing who was paying him and not caring as long as he got the money. That made things more difficult for David. He'd have to stake out the house and get hold of the suspect that way. It would have been a lot easier to find him at work or at home, but he didn't think that was going to happen.

David got home late that night. Kristen was practicing the piano and he could hear her before he walked in the door. He loved to listen to her play. He never had time for much music before. He liked what everybody else liked: the Beatles and the Rolling Stones. He liked the Moody Blues and Simon and Garfunkel, but he had never listened to classical music before. That was for old people. But now he had his favorites, which were mostly her favorites, because she played them all the time. And he realized that he loved them. He loved listening to Bach and Chopin. He wasn't too crazy about the modern composers, although he loved Debussy. But composers like Schoenberg were off his list entirely. He wanted something beautiful and easy to listen to.

Kristen was playing a Chopin that he particularly loved. He waited until she was finished, then walked in the door.

"It sounds beautiful, as usual."

She smiled. "Thank you. It's so wonderful to have someone who appreciates my playing. Most of the time I'm playing for myself. And I love my piano. It sounds so beautiful, even when I don't. When I was a postulant, Maribeth and Joan used to listen to me practice all the time. Too bad Maribeth tried to kill me. She really enjoyed my playing."

David laughed along with Kristen. "One minor flaw. Too bad she's not here anymore to listen."

"Yeah, it wouldn't be the same."

"I don't think you'd feel as comfortable."

Kristen got up from the piano.

"I actually fixed dinner! I hope you like ribs and coleslaw."

"Wow. That sounds wonderful. And I'm starving. It was a frustrating day."

"Okay, sit down and tell me all about it after I get everything on the table."

It was nice having Kristen home for summer vacation. Maybe they wouldn't have to go to Steak and Shake four times a week—at least, for a few months.

David told her about how he couldn't find Arthur Schmidt and couldn't even find out where he worked. But he also discovered that Schmidt was receiving money from someone.

"He probably doesn't have to work for a while, if someone's paying him enough to harass you—and me. I have to find out who's paying him. That's my next task. The list is still the same. Inez, Sister Janine from Franklin, Sister Jeanette, and Sister Hilda, although I'm not too worried about her. These ribs are delicious. How did you make them?"

"I baked them and put some barbeque sauce on them."

"You can make them any time. I'll never have to get another hamburger again."

"I can do this all summer, but when school starts up again, I'll teach you how to make them."

"I guess it's hamburgers and French fries in September, then. I'll enjoy the ribs for now, though." David kept talking. "It has to be someone with a lot of money, because they're paying Arthur enough money to live on just to threaten you."

"Or it could be their good friend, doing them a favor."

"Risking your life as a favor to a friend? I'm getting a search warrant tomorrow and going back to his house. I'm almost sure he's there at home. His mother didn't want to tell me."

"I hope you can find him soon. Those phone calls are frightening."

CHAPTER 12

The next morning, David returned to the house with a search warrant, and sure enough, Arthur was sleeping. His mother had no choice but to wake him up to speak to David.

Arthur's eyes were bloodshot, and he looked like he only had a few hours' sleep, if that much. He sat down on the living room sofa in his pajamas. His mother brought him a cup of coffee. She didn't offer David anything.

"You followed a woman on Highway 40 at least four times last month and tried to run her off the road," David said to Arthur. "I got the car's license plate, which was rented in your name from the rental company. Can you explain what you were doing and who put you up to it? And why are you receiving money at Hayes Auto from an unknown source? I have a search warrant, and if I don't get satisfactory answers, I'll have to bring you down to the station."

"I haven't done anything wrong. I never followed anybody on the highway."

"I have your license plate number and I saw what you did because I was following you."

"I wasn't trying to hurt her. She cut me off and I was just trying to teach her a lesson."

"Get your driver's license and ID. You're coming with me."

"Are you going to arrest me?"

"Yes. I'm charging you with vehicular assault. I'm going to read you your rights."

"I have to get my license and things from my room. And I need to get dressed."

"Don't try to leave from the back. I have another officer there."

★ ★ ★

David questioned Arthur at the station.

"Who's giving you the money?"

"I have no idea. My friend George brings the money every week to the shop where I just started working. He asked me a couple of months ago if I needed more money. I said sure, because the job at the security place was only part-time. He told me his friend needed to teach this woman a lesson and I wasn't supposed to hurt her, but just give her a scare. So I did that a few times, and then George would pay me with cash. I don't know where the money came from. Then I lost my job at the security place, and he helped me get this job now. He told me to call a number in the middle of the night, and I got paid for that too. But I can't get through to that number anymore and I told him that. So it's George you need to talk to."

"Don't worry, I will, but for now, you're staying here with us for a few nights. I have enough evidence to charge you with endangering someone's life."

David left the station and drove back out to Florissant. He figured that Arthur probably didn't know who was paying him. Whoever it was had been careful.

But he'd find out—and learn the connection—even though it wasn't clear right now. It could be anyone on the list that he and Kristen had drawn up.

CHAPTER 13

David pushed open the door at Hayes Auto.

"Can you call George again from the back?"

"Yes, sir." The secretary stood up quickly and walked to the back. "Hey, George," she yelled. "That cop is here again and wants to talk to you."

George walked through the door.

"Is there a place we can sit and talk?" David asked.

"Let's go in this office. Nobody's here right now."

When they were seated, David leaned forward. "Tell me about you and Arthur Schmidt."

George wiped his hands together nervously. "I've known him since high school, and he's always been in lots of trouble. I don't know how he got that job at that security company, but he did. They were crazy to hire him, but I guess he did an okay job for a while. I'm not surprised he got fired, though."

"What's this money he's getting and who's it from?"

"I don't know." George looked down at his hands and tried to rub a spot of grease off of them.

"Arthur told me everything. You don't have to hide it anymore. He told me about the man who gives you the money, and then you give it to Arthur. And also how you suggested Arthur for the job, so you're directly involved in this."

"I can't tell you who he's getting the money from. I'll lose my job if I do."

"You're going to be in even more trouble if you don't. I can arrest you for withholding evidence and bring you down to jail. We're talking some serious time."

George was quiet. Then he started talking.

"I have two jobs. They're both part-time. This one here, and my other job is as a maintenance person at this building in the city. There are a lot of businesses in the building. So one day, this lawyer from one of the law offices comes to me and says he needs a job done, and do I know anybody who has a car and some extra time. So I thought of Art and gave the guy his name. He contacted Arthur and didn't want anybody to know he was paying him, so he paid him in cash and asked me to give him the money."

"Who was the lawyer?"

"His name's Vincent Marino. He's a big hotshot lawyer, the head of one of those fancy law firms. When I found out how much he was paying Art, I complained to Mr. Marino, and he gave me a bonus to keep my mouth shut about it. He told me never to call him at his office, but I have his home number for emergencies. And I haven't told anyone, up till now."

"Did you ever call him at that number?"

"Yeah, I did, but just twice. Once when Art lost his job at the security company, and then when the phone calls to the number he gave us didn't work anymore."

"What number did he give you?"

"He wanted Art to call in the middle of the night and hang up on these people to annoy them. It wasn't hurting them or anything. Just annoying them. But then I guess they got a different number and I called Marino's home phone to tell him. Those were the only two times."

David could get the phone records and establish a connection between the three people involved, a tangible connection that couldn't be disputed in court.

CHAPTER 14

David and Officer Jackson walked into Vincent Marino's office. It had leather couches and chairs, beautiful Van Gogh prints on the walls, and an Oriental rug on the floor. His secretary asked if she could help them.

"St. Louis Police. We need to speak with Vincent Marino."

"Do you have an appointment?" she asked, according to the script.

"No, but we need to see him now. Can you please tell him we're here?"

She lifted the phone and dialed a number.

"Mr. Marino. Two policemen are here from the St. Louis Police Department, and they would like to speak with you." She paused. "Yes, sir, I'll tell them."

"He'll be right out. You can sit over there and wait for him." She pointed to the leather couch close to the office door.

A few minutes later, Marino came out of his office with a broad smile.

"Officer Kelly? It's good to see you again. How can I help you?"

David thought, You won't be thinking it's good to see me in a few minutes. How can you be so cheerful and so guilty at the same time?

A flicker of doubt crossed his mind.

"Mr. Marino—"

"Call me Vince, please."

"No, I'd rather call you Mr. Marino. Can we go in your office? We have a few more questions for you."

"Of course. Come on in." He led them into his office and gestured to two chairs. They sat down as he went back behind his large wooden desk.

"I still haven't heard anything from Jeanette. Have you?"

David responded neutrally, "I have some questions about that, Mr. Marino. Are you familiar with the name Arthur Schmidt?"

Marino looked sincerely perplexed. "No, I can't say I've ever heard the name before. Why do you ask?"

"We found out from him that you've been paying him money every week to harass and possibly injure the woman who helped me on Jeanette's case."

"What? I have no idea what you're talking about! I haven't given money to anybody."

"Do you know George Wright?"

"No, I have no idea who these people are. And I'm certainly not giving them money for anything. You can look at my check registers and find out for yourselves," he said angrily.

"You're going to have to tell me why you gave the money to this man, or else we'll have to take you down to the station and interview you there."

"I know my rights. You can't take me down there. I have a right to a lawyer. I am a lawyer."

"I realize that, but we're not arresting you for anything. We're merely trying to find the connection between you and these other men."

"There isn't any connection. I already told you that."

"In that case, you're going to have to come with us to be questioned."

"I know my rights. You know I won't say a word without my lawyer present."

"Do you want someone to come with you down to the station?"

"Yes." Marino picked up the telephone and dialed a number. "Gary, come to my office right now. Yes, it's important."

★ ★ ★

Interviewing Vincent Marino was exhausting. He knew too much about what to say and not say, a lot more than David knew. He knew that what Art said about the money wouldn't hold up in court, because there were no records of the money. He knew that the fact that he had asked George to find someone for him was also deniable. He could simply deny that he'd ever met either of them. There was no way to trace anything to him. Marino's mistake was to give George his number for an emergency, and for George to have called it. Now the police had a record of two calls to a private number from a person whom Vincent Marino claimed he had never even met. The calls weren't mistakes. They lasted almost five minutes each, and even though there was no record of what had been said, it was enough to prove they knew each other.

David was exhausted when he got home late. He had called Kristen late in the afternoon and told her not to wait up. When he came in the door, he found her asleep on the couch. Her book had slipped onto the floor, and she looked so beautiful, more so than anyone he had seen all day. But he tiptoed into the kitchen, determined not to wake her.

CHAPTER 15

I woke suddenly to the sound of the refrigerator door closing, and called, "David?"

"Hi, honey. I tried not to wake you."

"Don't worry. I'll get up and have dinner with you. I haven't eaten yet. You can tell me if anything happened today."

"You stay there. I'll get something."

"I have dinner in some bowls. You can heat them up."

"Okay. I see them."

We sat at the table eating the clam chowder I had fixed that morning.

"I love this. It tastes delicious," David said as he sat back and relaxed.

"Well, did anything happen?"

"You won't have to worry anymore. I have three people in custody, but I still have to collect more evidence. And you're so lucky you didn't get hurt."

"Tell me!"

"You know I can't tell you anything about an ongoing investigation, but if I were you, I wouldn't worry anymore about being run off the road, or phone calls in the middle of the night."

"You'll be able to tell me when the trial is over or the case is settled, right?"

"I think a judge will decide, not a jury. Of course, that's up to the defendant, and the courts, but the defendant can waive his right to a jury trial. I think he will. And it shouldn't take very long, not as long as those murder cases we were involved in. Just don't worry anymore. That's the important thing."

David was right about that. A huge weight had been lifted off me. I still had to worry about my classes in the fall, along with all the little ordinary things all people are concerned about, like my health, getting enough exercise, our relationship, whether I had made the right career choice, and planning our small wedding. But those things were nothing compared to what I had been so frightened of—someone seeking revenge and trying to kill me because of the investigations.

★ ★ ★

The summer went by quickly. David and I played tennis two or three times a week. I helped out at the orphanage with him every Friday and grew to love the children he worked with. I spent time with my parents, and we had dinner with them every Sunday. I knew what my classes were for the fall, and I prepared for them in the evenings, as well as practicing.

One Thursday at the end of August, David called and told me he would be late, so I waited to fix dinner until he got home. He walked in the door and took me in his arms.

"Let's go out tonight and celebrate."

"Okay. What are we celebrating?"

"I'll tell you at the restaurant."

He drove us to the Ritz-Carlton, and even though I wasn't dressed for it, we were welcomed like we belonged there.

After we sat down and ordered, David finally told me. "It's all over. The judge sentenced the three people in your case. I was pleased with the sentences they received. You won't be bothered anymore."

He told her about Arthur and George, and how Arthur had been the one following her.

"Was George the one paying him? And why?"

"No, you're never going to believe who was paying him. It was Vincent Marino."

"Jeanette's brother? The nice one? The one you talked to who didn't know where she was? The one who sent the stamps?"

"Yep. It was all a lie. He was doing it for her. He knew exactly where she was all the time and was willing to risk your life for her revenge."

"Wow."

"Remember how upset you were about Maribeth—how she deceived you, and you thought you were so gullible and naïve?"

"Well, I was. I think I've learned a lot since then."

"That's how *I* feel right now. I believed Marino. I thought he was a good, honest person who had somehow escaped his family's Mafia connections. It turns out he's as bad as the rest of them. And that's not the only thing he's done. Jeanette was the one who threatened him. She told him that unless he helped her, she'd tell the police about all the deals he had made and the money he had made from them. We're only beginning to work on the fraud from his law firm. I was too naïve and gullible to see what he was really like."

"Maybe it's not being naïve. Maybe it's being human. We always want to see the best in people."

"But I should know better. I deal with criminals every day. It makes me doubt almost every interaction I have with people."

I reached over and took his hand, which was large, strong, and tanned. I held it tightly.

I told him, "Maybe I've learned more than you have. I can be wrong about people. I'm not great at reading them—their motives or the way they think. As soon as I think I have someone figured out, they surprise me. Maybe it's not a bad problem to have."

"You know, you might be right. I've been thinking all this time that reading and understanding people was something I was good at. Maybe I should be a little more honest with myself, and admit I can make mistakes. A lot of them. I'm not very good at doing that either. It's been a lesson in humility that I needed."

"We all do."

We sat quietly for a few minutes, and finished our wine and our meal.

"Let's head home," David said quietly.

Both cats were asleep in the bedroom when we got there, an unusual moment of peace.

We sat on the couch, close together. JC woke up and wanted some petting. Alex was enjoying a much-needed nap in the other room.

I asked David, which was unusual because he usually asked me first, "What are you thinking about?"

"I was thinking about that book that Sister Mary Patrick wrote and wondering if she had any good ideas in it."

"Maybe," I said. "I'll need to discuss it with you in detail. We can start tomorrow, if you'd like."

"I always wanted to learn more about meditating, especially that kind. But let's not wait until tomorrow."

"I agree. JC, time for you to go to bed. David and I need to practice our 'meditation.' "

CONVENT MYSTERY #6

THE VINEYARD

CHAPTER 1

November 1971

Sister Carolyn was stationed at the convent in Defiance, Missouri. The building, constructed in the 1920s, was large, although there were very few nuns residing there. Originally, at the peak of Catholic education in the U.S, it had served as a grade school, high school, boarding school, and a separate convent, all within one expansive wing of the same structure.

A vineyard owned by the order once surrounded it, but it was sold in 1948 to a wealthy landowner, resulting in the sisters receiving no more income from the grapes or wine produced there. Sister Carolyn loved gazing out over the vast acres of Norton grapes, the best variety to grow in Missouri, and watching the hired workers in the fields tend to them throughout the year.

She had only been in Defiance a few months, since September, when the new school year began. The rules of her Catholic order had changed by 1971, and many sisters not only wore more modern habits but also used their birth names instead of the names that had been assigned to them. In the past, every nun had to "give up" her real name and choose the name of a saint upon taking her final vows. This was a symbol of her dedication to serving God. By the time Carolyn took her vows a few years ago, she could have kept her birth name, but there were too many nuns with variations on the name, such as Sister Mary Carolyn, Carolyn Marie, and so on, so she chose Sister Mary Patrick in honor of her grandfather. However, with a change of address and schools, she decided it was time to change her name as well, back to plain Sister Carolyn Johnston. She also changed her habit, opting for a navy-blue skirt, white blouse, and a veil that allowed a bit of brown hair to peek out from the front.

She sat in her small room with her pen in hand, making the final edits to the last chapter of her "meditation" book. Her room, like all the others in the convent, was sparsely furnished, featuring an old bed, a wooden dresser, and a desk that had been brought over from the school.

She didn't mind the sparse furnishings because she had a large window that looked out to the vineyards and she loved the view: the fog in the morning, the bright light at noon, the workers going up and down the rows of vines, the setting sun peeking through the rows. The view was peaceful every day. She had brought lace curtains from her other convent, a wonderful gift from some Irish friends. She had a nice typewriter and had managed to finish her entire book on it. She made only one copy, the one she had given to Kristen.

She thought about Kristen, the ex-nun she had met while stationed at her previous school last year.

Kristen had been practice-teaching there. She had an English degree and had been kicked out of the convent. That was the story Sister Carolyn heard, and she thought Kristen might be the perfect person to read her book. Kristen was surprised—more like shocked—when she realized the book wasn't about "meditation" at all, but rather an illicit romance between a nun and a priest.

Sister Carolyn remembered the day they discussed it. How could she ever forget? Kristen walked into the teacher's lounge during her free period when they had arranged to meet, but two teachers were already there.

"Sister Mary Patrick?"

"Yes?"

"Do you have time to talk about your manuscript?"

"Oh, yes, did you get a chance to read it?"

"Yes. I was a little surprised."

"I'll bet you were."

Sister Mary Patrick had looked around the room. "Let's go to my homeroom to talk. There's no one there right now."

"Good idea."

They'd walked silently down the corridor. Most of the students were in class. A few lingered by their lockers, looking for their books or talking during their free periods. Kristen and Sister Mary Patrick went into the empty classroom, closed the door, and sat at two students' desks.

Kristen had been surprised, but said she enjoyed the book a lot more than a book on meditation, especially after she had spent a year in the convent. Kristen had asked her why she wrote it and Sister Mary Patrick had been honest. "I want to leave, and I hope that if I can get this published, I can make a little money. My family can't help. I know I won't make much, but it might be enough to get started. That's one reason I asked you to read it, because you've already left and would understand."

"Please don't show it to anyone!" Sister Mary Patrick had begged.

Kristen apologized quickly. "I've already shared parts of it with David, my fiancé. I hope that's okay."

"That's fine. Just don't show it to anyone else."

"Don't worry, I won't. I promise. He really liked it too. Are you going to use a pen name when you publish it?"

"I'm going to have to. I can't publish it under my real name. That wouldn't look very good, would it?"

"What name will you use?"

"Something sexy. Help me think of something."

"Me? I have no idea." Kristen had laughed. "I don't read many romance novels!"

"You should. We can think of something together."

"How about Tiffany, or Candy, or Diamond?"

"I like Candy."

"How about Candy Cane?"

"That's stupid."

They had both started laughing, but stopped as a few students came in the door for their math class.

"Okay, how about Tiffany? And you could use a color. Blue—like in jazz—the blues."

"I like that. Tiffany Blue. Okay, I'll use it."

"Well, that was easy." Kristen laughed.

"It won't matter anyway. It'll probably never get published."

"Don't say that. Your book is amazing. My boyfriend and I loved it. I think it's going to be really popular."

"Thanks. I sure hope so."

CHAPTER 2

Sister Carolyn had a lot to lose if it came out that she wrote a romance novel. She could get kicked out of the convent before she was ready to leave and get in lots of trouble at the high school where she was teaching. Kristen had promised she wouldn't say a word and Sister Carolyn hoped she would keep her promise.

She had been transferred at the end of the school year. She wasn't happy about the transfer but figured it wouldn't matter if she was leaving. It had been a hectic time with moving, and she suddenly realized that Kristen probably didn't even know she had been transferred—or had changed her name. She'd have to call her tomorrow. And she had great news because she had finally heard from a publisher who was excited about publishing her book and offered her an advance. It was tiny, but it was real money! She had filled out all the paperwork and was going to have them mail the money to a P.O. Box that she had set up at the Defiance post office. She even used the pen name they had come up with that day. However, she had to use her real name for the IRS. The old convent would still get the tax form from the publisher at the end of the year. They could send it to her new address or wherever she might be. But she couldn't tell anyone yet. That was the worst part. She was so excited and ready to start a new life, but couldn't share it with anyone, not even her family. Her mom would be so upset about the nature of the book that Sister Carolyn wasn't in any hurry to tell her. And her sister wouldn't ever know about it.

She finished her typing for the day and placed the papers in the bottom drawer of her desk. It was getting late in the afternoon, and she wanted to arrive at Ramon's house before Vespers. Ramon was the foreman of the vineyard. He was married to a beautiful woman named Juanita, and they had a lovely eight-year-old daughter named Maria. Ramon was Mexican, like most of the other workers there. Sister Carolyn enjoyed walking through the vineyard to think and to escape the confines of the convent, where she ran into Ramon one day.

He was a bit older than Sister Carolyn but had extensive knowledge about managing a vineyard. His parents and family owned a few vineyards in central Missouri, giving him plenty of experience. Plus, he was attractive. He had dark features, with straight black hair pulled back into a ponytail. He had politely asked her if she needed anything, and they started chatting a little. She encountered him more frequently, usually every afternoon in the vineyard. He was always working in the same area—she occasionally wondered why—and he likely questioned why she always took the same route in the late afternoon.

Meeting him became almost a daily ritual. One day, he took her to meet his wife and daughter, and the four of them visited for a long time. Sister Carolyn found the other nuns too stuffy and old and was glad to meet younger and more interesting people. Maria was almost nine years old, and when she discovered that Sister Carolyn wanted to learn Spanish, she was excited to teach her. They played games together in Spanish, and Sister Carolyn was learning a lot—and having fun.

One day, Ramon asked Sister Carolyn to come back to the house with him. As they neared the old ranch house, Ramon told her that Juanita and Maria were at the doctor for a checkup.

"I hope you don't mind."

Sister Carolyn said, "Of course not."

It was only one kiss—a long one. And they both loved it, but Sister Carolyn couldn't do that to Juanita and Maria, and Ramon realized just how close they were getting to something they couldn't control, so they stopped before anything else happened.

Ramon walked Sister Carolyn back through the vineyard. Neither one of them said anything about what had just happened. It was too soon and too beautiful for them both. But she knew they had to be careful.

CHAPTER 3

This evening, she walked to Ramon and Juanita's house. Juanita was there making dinner and Maria jumped up, excited to see her. "Can we play a game, *por favor*?"

"Oh, I wish we could, but I only stopped by to say hello. I have to get back for prayers. Tomorrow I'll come earlier, I promise."

Maria sulked a little, her long black hair covering her eyes, and whined, "You promise?"

"Yes, I do."

Ramon turned to Sister Carolyn. "Do you want me to walk you back home? It's getting dark?"

"No, I'm fine. It isn't quite dark yet, and I know my way. It's simple, a straight line"—she laughed— "but I'd better leave now."

He walked her to the door and watched as she disappeared down the path between the tall vines before he turned back to his family.

The vineyard lay dark in the twilight, yet it was peaceful. The sounds of frogs, crickets, and cicadas created a constant background noise. The moon was full and beautiful as it rose, peeking through at the end of each long row of vines. She gazed at the vines. The grapes would be ready for harvest in a few more weeks. It was a wonderful time of year. With Thanksgiving week approaching, school would be out in a few days. And then Christmas. The year was passing quickly. She hoped to be out of here and an independent woman sometime in the new year, if that was possible.

She thought about Ramon. She had to be very careful. She couldn't keep seeing him, yet she couldn't stop either. He had a wife and child, but she found herself falling in love with him. She planned to leave as soon as the book was published, but she wouldn't be living with Ramon; he already had a life of his own. He had kissed her first, but she had kissed him back, and loved the feel of his lips on hers. She thought about him often during the day, but what was she going to do? She hoped to make enough money to possibly rent a small apartment and secure a teaching job somewhere else in the state. She held a Missouri teaching credential for high school, so it shouldn't be too difficult. Teachers were always in demand.

She heard a noise behind her. It wasn't the frogs or cicadas. The workers had all gone home. It was probably Ramon's black lab, Reina, wandering freely through the vineyards.

Sister Carolyn turned and called, "Reina, is that you? Come here, girl."

The dog usually ran right up to her, wagging her tail and licking her hand.

Maybe it was Ramon...

Suddenly a figure appeared in the twilight off to her left. Sister Carolyn was relieved. "Oh, it's you. Thank God. You scared me. What are you doing here?"

A moment before the shovel came down on her head, she screamed, "What are you doing?"

But she was no match for the force of the shovel and the swiftness of the attack. She fell quickly, the blood pouring from her head. The person threw the shovel on the ground and watched as Sister Carolyn's eyes closed for the last time. They felt for a pulse but couldn't find one. They pulled off their gloves, threw them on the ground, took a last look around in the remaining light, and walked down the path between the thick vines.

CHAPTER 4

"Sister Carolyn missed Vespers again today. That's a whole week in a row," Sister Henrietta whispered to Sister Gloria, the superior of the convent, as they walked from the chapel into the refectory for dinner.

"I know," Sister Gloria said. "I'll talk to her about it." It really wasn't any of Sister Henrietta's business. But Sister Henrietta was retired and in her late seventies and didn't have much to do except worry and gossip about other people's problems.

Sister Gloria didn't want to make Sister Henrietta feel bad, as that would create another problem she'd have to deal with. She tried to sound understanding and appreciative that Henrietta brought up the subject.

Everyone was at dinner, five of them, except for Sister Carolyn. At one time the sisters staffed all the schools, but now most of the teachers were lay teachers, and very few nuns taught at the school.

Sister Gloria was the superior of the convent and taught social studies in high school; Sister Martin taught fifth grade, Sister Angeline taught first grade, Sister Henrietta was the cook and housekeeper for the convent, and Sister Emma taught mathematics in high school. Sister Carolyn taught high-school religion, but had a degree in biology.

After ten o'clock that evening, Sister Gloria knocked on Sister Carolyn's door, but there was no answer. Sister Carolyn hadn't attended Vespers or dinner, and Sister Gloria hadn't seen her all day, now that she thought about it. This wasn't particularly unusual, as Sister Carolyn was very solitary and had only been stationed there a few months. She spent a lot of time in her room. Someone had mentioned she was writing a book, but Sister Carolyn never spoke of it, and Sister Gloria had never seen any evidence of a manuscript. She couldn't recall who had mentioned it, and Sister Carolyn had never discussed it.

Sister Gloria checked in the small chapel, but no one was there, so she headed to her room for the night. As she closed her door and took off her veil, she heard pounding on the front door and the doorbell ringing repeatedly. It was almost eleven. This was not acceptable! She quickly put her veil back on, tucking her hair underneath, and stomped down the corridor to the heavy wooden front door.

She didn't dare open it but eyed the telephone by the door in case she needed to call the police. She realized burglars wouldn't knock, but her heart was still beating quickly. Sister Angeline came up behind her, clutching her robe, trying to cover her ample body, clearly wondering what was happening.

"Who is it?" Sister Gloria called loudly.

"It's Ramon, sister. Open up. It's an emergency."

She knew Ramon, and the voice sounded like his. But to make sure, she stood on her tiptoes and peered through the tiny peephole.

It was Ramon, with an anxious look on his face, holding his hat with both hands nervously.

She opened the door.

"Sister, it's Sister Carolyn. She's dead. She's been murdered. Call the police right now!"

"Dead? What are you talking about?"

"Call the police right now. I came here right away. Call them now."

Sister Gloria stood there in shock. Ramon walked in, pushing her aside, and grabbed the phone by the front door.

"I'll call them." He dialed 911 and handed the phone to Sister Gloria.

She took the phone and said, "Yes, I'd like to report a death, a murder." She paused. "Priory Lane. Defiance."

"Please send someone right away. The address is 9173 Priory Lane. It's the convent by the vineyard. Yes, someone will be here." She hung up the phone. "What happened?" she asked Ramon.

"I was doing my last rounds in the vineyard like I always do, and I found her lying on the ground, with blood all around her head. She's dead. I felt her wrist for a pulse but there wasn't one. You have to come with me, now."

Sister Gloria ran back to her room, and on the way, told Sister Angeline, who was hiding in the shadows, to wake up all the nuns and take them to the front parlor. She dressed quickly and walked quickly back to the front door, where she met Ramon, who led the way through the vineyard. He had a flashlight and knew exactly where he was going. Sister Gloria saw Sister Carolyn's body on the ground and the blood around her head. She couldn't breathe. This couldn't be happening.

Ramon said, "Don't touch anything. The police will want everything the way I found her. But I wanted you to see her body before anyone else came."

Sister Gloria made the sign of the cross and tried to say a prayer but couldn't even think of anything to ask God. She was suddenly angry at Him. Why had He permitted this? Sister Carolyn was a good person who seemed to care very much about other people. God always seemed to choose the wrong people to die. Sister Gloria turned around and tried not to think any more blasphemous thoughts. "I have to be back when the police get there."

"I'll go with you to light the way."

"Thank you."

They walked back in silence. The police car was already out in front of the convent. Two policemen were getting out.

Ramon went up to them. "I can take you to her."

The officer gestured to Sister Gloria. "Who are the two of you?"

"I'm Sister Gloria, the superior of the convent."

"My name is Ramon Munros. I'm the foreman of the vineyard. I discovered the body of Sister Carolyn about a half hour ago."

"Can you take us to the body?"

"Of course," Ramon answered.

"Do you need me to come?" Sister Gloria asked.

"Yes," said the first policeman.

Ramon and Sister Gloria retraced their steps through the vineyard.

"We have to get there before the irrigation goes on at night," Ramon said. "We have to hurry."

"How much time do we have?" the policeman asked as he walked faster.

Ramon glanced at his watch. "Only about ten minutes, sir."

"Can you turn off the irrigation?" the policeman asked.

"I don't think I'll have time. It's at the far end of the vineyard and I'll have to go back and get my car and drive down there..."

The policeman interrupted him, "You and I will have to move her body. I hate to do that, but we'll have to."

"Of course," Ramon said quickly.

The policeman took pictures of the scene with his Polaroid camera, and Ramon shined his flashlight. They worked quickly and then carefully picked up the body.

"We can bring her over to one of the sheds by the side. It'll be dry and we can put her body there," Ramon said.

"The coroner will be here as soon as he can, but I think this has to be done now."

Ramon looked at her body after they put her gently down on one of the tables in the shed. He couldn't believe this had happened. He had kissed her. He loved her, but he couldn't act like he did. He had to act like she was just one of the nuns, no one special to him. He felt like crying inside. He would do that later, when he was alone. He couldn't do it now.

"You two go back to the convent. I'm going to stay with the body until the coroner arrives, Sister. You both need to be questioned by Sargeant Hoffman, along with the other sisters."

"Yes, sir," Ramon answered quickly. "I'll walk you back there, Sister Gloria."

★ ★ ★

Sister Gloria and Ramon returned and went into the main parlor with the other policemen to talk to the nuns gathered there.

The older officer, Hoffman, had a lot of questions for them that he had already asked the other sisters.

"When did you last see Sister Carolyn?" "Was she at dinner tonight?" "Was it unusual for her to be out in the orchard this late at night?"

Since they were only the two officers in the small police department, they needed someone who did homicide investigations. It was very early in the morning, just past one, when Detective Kelly arrived at the scene of the murder. He talked mostly to the officers and the coroner before the body was taken away and told the sisters that he would return the next day to question them.

CHAPTER 5

David got a phone call in the middle of the night. I woke up in a panic, thinking that whole horrible experience of people waking us up at three in the morning was going to start over again. But then I heard him on the phone in the kitchen, and I realized he was actually speaking to someone. He came back into the bedroom and saw I was awake.

"Police business. I'll be back as soon as I can. You go back to sleep. I'll lock the door. Don't worry. Love you."

I think I said goodbye to him, but I turned over in bed and fell back asleep until morning. By then, he was sound asleep next to me, and I didn't dare wake him. I had no idea when he had gotten back or gone to sleep.

I fed the cats, who meowed loudly about their lack of food when they saw me and I didn't want their meowing to wake David.

"Okay, okay, I'm going as fast as I can," I told them as I opened a can of wet food and dumped it into their bowls. The meowing stopped immediately, thank God. They could be loud.

I sat and read the paper and fixed myself some cereal. It was Thanksgiving week, and I had nowhere to go. It was a glorious feeling, after two months of teaching, to wake up in the morning and know I could go back to sleep if I wanted—at least, for a few days.

I finally heard David get up. He made his way out to the kitchen, looking exhausted.

"Good morning, love," I said. "You had a late night?"

"I had to drive out all the way to Defiance for a murder investigation."

"Defiance? That's over an hour away. It's out of your jurisdiction, isn't it?"

"Yeah, but they only have two officers on their police force, and no one who has the experience to investigate a murder, so they called us. I got the lucky phone call."

"I'm sorry. You must be exhausted."

"I am. And guess what? It's another nun."

"What? No, not really?"

"Yes, I hope you don't know anyone in Defiance."

"Thank God, no. I've hardly even heard of the place. Our order doesn't staff it, that's for sure."

"Good, I'm glad. I am sorry she was killed, though. It sounds pretty simple. We should be able to solve this one easily."

"I hope so. Are you going back out there today?"

"Yeah, I have to. I'll be gone for most of the day. You have any plans?"

"Nope. I'm going to relax. Maybe go shopping with Pam or a few other friends. Maybe I'll have lunch with Louise. That's it. I'm going to enjoy my few days off."

"Good. You deserve it."

David left soon after breakfast for Defiance and I spent the day relaxing and planning the next few days of my wonderful vacation time. We were invited to my parents for Thanksgiving. I would bring a dish, but Mom would do most of the cooking, which she loved. I had invited a few friends and David had asked if he could bring two friends from the police department. Mom and Dad were always excited to meet new people, so we would have at least twelve people at dinner on Thursday.

* * *

We had a wonderful Thanksgiving. I was beginning to get used to my teaching schedule. I had gotten a job only about fifteen minutes away from our apartment at Maplewood High School. I was teaching freshman and sophomore English and was starting to enjoy it. I overprepared every lesson plan, and the students didn't really learn what I wanted them to learn, but I was gradually paying more attention to the students instead of how well I thought I was teaching. It made all the difference in the world.

The first few tests made me realize I needed to pay attention to what the students were actually learning. There were even a few times we had good discussions in the classroom.

CHAPTER 6

Christmas

I missed seeing Michael. He had called, but we put off meeting for coffee. The time was never quite right. He called again in early December, and we decided to get together, no more excuses. We met at a Walgreens by the mall close to our houses.

We hugged each other, and I realized how much I had missed him.

"Why haven't we gotten together before this?" he asked.

"I don't know. We live so close to each other. Let's not be strangers." I didn't want to see him that often, because I liked him a little too much.

I was the first to ask, "How's your teaching going?"

"I'm fine. Same as always. The real question is, how are *you* doing? Your first year on your own!" He seemed genuinely interested.

"I love it. I love teaching my two freshman classes. The sophomores are a little crazy. I'm hoping to get a senior class next year. They seem to be a lot more serious about studying—getting into college is important to a lot of them, and they seem to relate to the questions in literature more than the younger ones."

"I guess that's true. And I'm glad you're liking it so much."

I asked him about some of the people at the school where I'd done my practice teaching. I was especially interested in Sister Mary Patrick, even though he wouldn't know anything about her book.

"How's Sister Mary Patrick? I haven't talked to her since last June, and I've meant to call her and see how she's doing."

Michael was silent, his expression blank as he stared at me.

"You haven't heard what happened?"

"What do you mean? Heard what?"

"Oh, my God. I'm so sorry to be the one to tell you. She got transferred in August to a school in Defiance, Missouri, and she was killed just a month ago, in November."

"Killed? She couldn't have been. My fiancé is working on a case out there, but that's not the name of the sister."

"When she got transferred, she changed back to her old name, her birth name, which was Carolyn."

I sat with my cup of hot chocolate, not knowing what to say. My hand started shaking. I put the cup down. Sister Mary Patrick was dead, and I hadn't known anything about it. I felt sick. I started to cry.

He put his hand on mine. Just a friend helping another friend.

"Michael, I'm sorry, but I have to go. I can't believe this. We need to do this some other time. I really want to talk to you, but I can't believe she's dead."

Michael didn't let go of my hand. "I'm so sorry. I had no idea the two of you were so close. And I thought you knew about her death. I completely understand. Here, let me pay. You go on ahead. Call me in a week or so and we'll try this again. Okay?"

"Yes," I said, not even sure of what I was saying. We stood up. He hugged me and I hugged him back, holding him tightly, tears in my eyes.

I drove home, sat with the cats, and waited until David walked in the door. He smiled and picked up Alex as soon as he came in the door. "How's my cutie?"

"I have something to tell you. Something important."

He put the cat down, took off his uniform jacket, and hung it up on the coat rack. Then he sat down next to me.

"What is it? You look pretty upset."

"The sister in Defiance that you're investigating. Sister Carolyn?"

"Yes?"

"I told you I didn't know anyone there. Well, Sister Carolyn is Sister Mary Patrick, the one I practice taught with and the one who wrote the romance book that we read."

"I don't understand what you're saying."

"Sister Mary Patrick got transferred last summer—I didn't know that—and when she got transferred, she decided to change her name back to her original name of Carolyn. I didn't know that either, because I hadn't talked to her since last June."

"What do you mean, changed her name? How can nuns just change their names?"

"We take different names when we take our vows, to show God we're giving up everything. At that time, she took, or was given, the name Mary Patrick. But with the rules changing, she probably decided it was time to go back to her original birth name, which was Carolyn."

"She was the one who wrote the romance book that we read? Oh, my God."

"Yeah, and I feel terrible that she was murdered. You never found anything like her manuscript during your investigation?"

"No, not a thing. I would have known right away if I had seen anything like that. But there was nothing. Nothing at all. No notes or letters from publishers or anything. Just some teaching plans and religion books. That was it."

"I wonder what happened to all her stuff. That manuscript might be a reason someone killed her."

"Now, don't go down that path. There's no reason to think that."

"Okay, but I wonder what happened to all her writing? It can't have simply disappeared."

"Well, it's something I'll be investigating, that's for sure. I'm so sorry the victim was your friend. I had no idea. How did you find out?"

"I met with Michael today at that Walgreens down the street. We started talking, and I asked him about Sister Mary Patrick. He looked shocked and told me she had been murdered. Then he recounted the whole story. I was so upset that I left, telling him we'd have to meet again sometime. I couldn't stay and discuss school and students after hearing that. He understood."

"Yeah, he still teaches at her former school, doesn't he, so I guess he would know all about it—and the change of names and everything."

I had to ask David, "I know you can't tell me much, but how's the investigation going? Have you found out what happened to her?"

"You know I can't talk about that. We do have a suspect, but I'm not entirely convinced. I have to check out a few more things."

"You're going to tell me to stay out of this, but you should really try to find her manuscript. It can't have disappeared. It was too important to her. It was her ticket to get out of the convent and start a whole new life."

"Don't worry, now that I know who she is and that she wrote that book, you can be sure I'm going to follow up on that. You're right; it can't have vanished."

"I guess I have the only copy of it now. Too bad she never had the chance to publish it and leave her order. That was her dream."

"I'll let you know as much as I can about the investigation, but it won't be very much. I'm sorry this happened to a friend of yours. I hope this is the very last time it happens."

He held me in his arms for a long time, until JC got so obnoxious about getting between us that we finally gave up and petted the cat for a while.

CHAPTER 7

I called Michael after Christmas. I was glad he had waited for me to call him.

"Hey, Michael, did you have a nice Christmas?"

"It was wonderful. I got together with my family, my mom, sisters and brothers. We had a great, crazy time. How are you? I felt so bad about telling you about Sister Mary Patrick the other day."

"I'm glad you did. I would have found out sooner or later. It was such a shock, though. I know you understood. Do you want to meet again for coffee?"

"I'd love to. Same place? How about sometime next week after school?"

We met on a Tuesday afternoon. I got to Walgreens early and found a little table. The waitress came up to me and asked what I wanted. I told her a hot chocolate.

She hesitated, then said to me, "Honey, I want to tell you something. I waited on you last time you were here."

I looked up at her. I remembered her. She was in her mid-fifties, with a stocky build and a pleasant face. I wondered what she could possibly want to tell me.

"I saw you with your boyfriend last time you were here, and I want to tell you to be careful. I mean, it's fine that you have a cup of coffee with somebody like that, but you sure got some funny looks when he held your hand and you guys started hugging. People were really staring at you. I'd be careful, if I were you."

"Well, first of all, he's not my boyfriend, and he'd just told me about the death of someone we both knew. He was trying to help me feel better."

"I'm not judging you, honey. I'm saying be careful, that's all."

She turned around and went back to the counter.

I sat there, angry at myself for making any excuses about our behavior. Yes, he was trying to make me feel better, but what if he were my boyfriend? So what? I could have a Black boyfriend, and he could have a white girlfriend! There wasn't anything wrong with that. But for many people, there was a lot wrong with it. I hated racist people. My parents were from Ireland, and even though they were as white as possible, they never once said anything disparaging about anyone of any other race. Never in my whole life. They had their opinions about politicians, but never about anyone because of the color of their skin.

She brought my coffee as Michael arrived. He looked great. He gave me a hug and he sat down and ordered coffee. I didn't say a word to him about what the waitress had said, but we started talking about the murder right away.

"Nobody at school could believe what happened. I guess she got killed by the man who was in charge of the vineyard. But no one seems to know why."

I didn't know how much I should share with Michael about the investigation. David didn't have any other suspects, but he felt increasingly unsure that the man in charge of the vineyards had murdered Sister Carolyn. He'd tried to find anything about the book she had written, but he couldn't get any information about it at all. I guess I had the only copy in the world. I felt bad, because it would have been a fun book for people to read. Not inspirational like a book on meditation, but it was a great romance book.

★ ★ ★

After the Walgreens incident, I suggested that Michael and I meet for coffee every month at the little Middle Eastern bakery halfway between our apartments. I really liked him as a friend, nothing more. Oh, it could have been more if I wanted it to be. I didn't know how to handle my feelings about men. I loved David, and I hadn't loved anyone else. My attempt to date other people had ended badly, and I realized how good David was, but Michael was incredibly nice too. We had a lot of fun together, and he was genuinely interested in me and my teaching. My parents would have had a heart attack if I ever brought him home as a boyfriend. A friend from school, a fellow teacher, was acceptable, but anything else was not. It was 1972 now, and I couldn't believe that racism still existed in our country. When were we going to get over this ridiculous notion that the color of someone's skin made any difference at all?

Anyway, I was, or tried to be, perfectly content with David. I tried not to think about Michael except as a good friend. And I couldn't tell if he was interested in me as anything more than a friend. He seemed very interested in everything I did and what I thought, and he was such fun to be with, and it seemed like he was interested in me, but he never did anything that would be disrespectful to my relationship with David. He never held my hand or kissed me or anything like that. I was glad, because I didn't know what I would have done.

I told David about what the waitress had said at Walgreens and how I decided to go somewhere else for coffee from then on. David understood completely.

"I run into that all the time at work. I'm not saying all cops are racist, but a lot of them are. It's pretty awful, and I don't fit in with the crowd, with their jokes and snide remarks. I try to ignore them."

"Why aren't you like that? I'm curious why some people are so racist while others aren't. My family wasn't like that at all. Well, maybe a little. They're all for civil rights, but if I brought Michael home as a boyfriend, I don't think they'd be pleased."

David was understanding. "I can see that. It would be difficult to be married to someone from another race. There's a lot of cultural differences, and the kids might have a hard time. Maybe that's why your parents are like that."

David went on. "You know all the trouble I had with my family: the arguments, the divorce, and all the problems I faced growing up. I was raised by my Irish grandparents, who came directly from Ireland and were treated very badly for being Irish. Of course, they were white, so it became easier to assimilate into society over time, but they never forgot about their oppression. My Grandpa Kelly often spoke about how sorry he was for those who faced prejudice. It truly bothered him. I guess that's what I learned when I was young, and I've never forgotten that lesson."

★ ★ ★

In June, school was finally over for the year. My first year of teaching was finished. My contract was already signed for the next fall at the same school. I was even getting a raise, although not very much. I was looking forward to the summer so much. I hoped David could take a little time off, but Ramon's trial was coming up in a few weeks, and David was desperately trying to find more evidence that would show that Ramon was not the murderer. So far he hadn't found anything beyond what they had discovered those first few days after the murder. He was getting more and more frustrated as the trial approached.

CHAPTER 8

Imade a special trip to the bookstore at the mall the Friday morning after school was over. I didn't have much to spend, but figured I would look for something fun to read. I was tired of lesson plans and great literature. Maybe I'd find something I couldn't get at the library. I checked out the display in the front section featuring the bestsellers. A book called *Defiant Love* caught my eye. Well, it was the cover that caught my eye: two scantily clad lovers embracing—a typical romance novel. But the author was Tiffany Blue. Oh, my God. That was the name Sister Mary Patrick and I had picked out for her last year. My hand was shaking as I reached for the book. I opened it and read the first page. It was word for word the same as Sister Mary Patrick's manuscript! Not the first page about meditation, but the second page that began the sexy part! She had somehow published the book before she died. I grabbed a copy, then reached back, grabbed another one, and went to the checkout counter.

I asked the girl there for the manager.

"Is anything wrong?" she asked. She was about my age, in her early twenties, and she looked very concerned.

"No. I have a few questions about this book."

"I'll get the manager. He's in the back. Hold on." She lifted the phone and dialed a number.

"This is Jane. There's someone out here who would like to speak to you. Okay, thanks."

She turned back to me. "He'll be out in a second."

"Thanks."

I waited after I paid for the books. The manager, an older, thin man with grey hair, came out shortly with a worried look.

"Hi," I said. "I was wondering how long you've been selling this book, and how well it's doing. A friend of mine wrote it, and I'm curious."

He looked relieved that I wasn't going to complain about the contents.

"We've been selling it since November. It's our fourth order from the publisher. It's quite a bestseller. I don't know how well it's doing in our other stores, but here it's doing great."

"Do you know anything about the author?"

"No. It looks like she used a pen name. There isn't any information about her in the book, not even a picture. That's about all I can tell you."

"Thanks. I appreciate it."

"You're welcome. I hope you enjoy it." He turned around and walked back toward his office, and I left the store with my two books in a plastic bag.

I drove directly home. David wasn't there yet, so I pulled out the manuscript and carefully compared the first few pages of both it and the book. It was the same, except for a few editorial changes, like quotation marks, periods in different places, and a few changes in sentence structure. Things an editor would catch when they were proofreading a manuscript. Other than that, they were the same.

I heard David at the door. JC and Alex did too. They both ran to the door, always trying to get out to explore the world.

"No, no, you stay inside," David said. "It isn't as great out there as you think, guys. You don't realize how nice you have it." David made it into the house and closed the door quickly, putting his briefcase down. He picked up Alex first and petted him, then JC for equal time.

"Hi, sweetie. Ready for the weekend?"

"Sit down," I told him. "I have something to show you."

"Okay. Can I get a drink first?"

"Sure, get me one too."

David came back from the kitchen with two Dr. Peppers and handed one to me. "Okay, show me what you have."

I handed him the book without saying anything.

He looked at the title, which meant nothing to him. Then I could see him read the author's name with a puzzled look on his face. He opened the book and started reading. After about a minute, he looked up at me.

"This is Sister Mary Patrick's book! Where did you get this?"

"I just bought it this afternoon."

"How did you find out about it?"

"I didn't. I mean, I had no idea. I saw it on the table in the bookstore where they put the bestsellers, and I recognized her pen name, the silly one we came up with last year. She used it, but the title must have been because she'd moved to Defiance."

"So she did get it published! I wonder when?"

"I don't know. I talked to the manager at the bookstore, and he said they've had to reorder it a number of times since November, so it's been at least six months."

David said, "I wonder who's collecting the royalties. And if they're going to the convent, they should have told us about that. It's important to the investigation. I'll have to ask the sisters— and her family."

"This might be the reason someone killed her." I had said that once before, and David had dismissed the idea. But not now.

"You know, you might be right. Now that you've found out it's been published and making some money, that could be a reason. I'll have to talk to the publisher." He turned the book over. "Sunrise Press. They're in New York, like most publishing companies. We can find out from them where they're sending the royalties."

"Maybe it wasn't Ramon who killed her."

"I hope not. I have this feeling—I've had it all along—that it wasn't him, but there's no evidence linking anyone else to the murder, and I've been wrong about people before. That incident with Marino really taught me a lesson about trusting people. I'm sure glad you found this book today."

"I am too. But it makes me doubly sad that Sister Mary Patrick- Carolyn, couldn't enjoy seeing her book in print, or be able to do all the things she wanted to do in her life."

David leaned over and kissed me. "I don't ever want to lose you. I've come so close too many times. I hope that never happens again."

I didn't answer because kissing was so much nicer than talking.

★ ★ ★

The next day, David called the publisher in New York and told me about it when he got home that evening.

"I talked to them, but it didn't help all that much. I asked to speak to the editor in charge of her book, but she's on a book tour in Europe for the next month and won't be back until September. It would be almost impossible to reach her. But I did talk to someone who told me the royalty checks were being sent to a P.O. box in Defiance, Missouri, and that they were being cashed every month. She didn't have an answer to how much money had been paid out, but they're very pleased with how well the book has been doing. She said they would get back to me about the amount that's been paid so far. That's all she could tell me."

"So someone's been getting the checks and cashing them. And nobody told you anything about that when you investigated her murder and asked the sisters about her?"

"No. And it means someone knows about her book and is cashing the checks, but it doesn't mean that person murdered her."

I wasn't convinced. "It sounds like a pretty good motive to me."

"Yes, it does, but one that would be hard to prove in court. Just because somebody knew about her book and is taking advantage of her publishing windfall, although that's illegal, it still doesn't mean they murdered her."

"I guess not."

"But we don't have much evidence on Ramon either, except that he found the body and was the last person to see her alive. It's easy to pin the murder on him, though, and that's what everyone wants to do. It's the simplest solution."

CHAPTER 9

June 1972

"There's a conference in Chicago next week that I'm going to for five days, a police conference," David informed me. "You're welcome to come with me, but frankly, I think you'd be bored. I'll be in meetings all day, and then probably more meetings in the evening. Do you know anybody in Chicago that you'd like to visit?"

"No, thanks. I'll stay here and entertain the cats and spend some time with Mom and Dad now that school is out. I haven't been able to do that in a while."

"Are you sure? I don't want you to feel like I'm leaving you out of anything. I'm going to the orphanage on Friday, and I'm off work Saturday. Can you take me to the airport Sunday morning?"

"Sure, and don't worry, I'll be fine."

"I hate to go right before the trial is about to begin, but I have to give a presentation there, so I can't skip it. And I need to get out to those two convents and find out if they know anything about the book. I guess I'll do that when I get back."

David was scheduled to leave Sunday morning, so I called Mother Hannah on Thursday and asked to make an appointment on Friday, the next day, to see her. She was the head of the order that Sister Mary Patrick (Carolyn) had belonged to.

I drove to their motherhouse in Florissant and sat in the parlor outside her office. Their motherhouse wasn't anything like ours. It was two old brick buildings that probably had a total of seven bedrooms between them. That was the total number of sisters they had studying in their order. I couldn't believe they'd been able to stay in existence.

She walked out and asked me to come into her office. She didn't look very friendly, and I had a feeling she wasn't going to like my idea at all. She probably thought I was here to ask about a vocation to religious life. Their order didn't have a college connected with its motherhouse, like ours did, so most nuns entered after getting their education elsewhere.

"Good afternoon, Kristen. I hope you're considering joining our order. If I can answer any questions, please let me know."

"No, I'm sorry, I didn't come here today for that reason. I have a request to make. As you know, one of your sisters was murdered last year in Defiance, and her alleged murderer is going to trial this month. My fiancé is the detective on the case, and he's very concerned they have the wrong person. We're very sure the murderer is one of the sisters at the convent at Defiance. I really hate to say that, but I think it's true."

Mother Hannah looked angry. "I can't believe that for a second. I assume you have no evidence of this, or you wouldn't be coming to me for help. And if you think I have any evidence of this, you're very much mistaken. The police have investigated very thoroughly. They've found nothing that would implicate any of us. In fact, I'd like you to leave right now. You have a lot of nerve coming here and asking me about this." She started to stand up.

"Please, at least let me explain why I think that."

"I have no idea who you are, and I don't know where you came up with your story, but if you expect me to believe it, you're wrong."

"It isn't a story I just 'came up with.' It's a very real possibility, and the police are investigating it right now. The problem is that the trial starts very soon, so this all has to be done quickly."

"And one of the detectives happens to be your fiancé? A likely story. Here's the phone. Why don't you call his station and let me speak to him? Better yet, I'll call his office and speak to him myself."

I froze. That was the last thing I needed. I hadn't expected her to be so skeptical. But she was right. I had to have some evidence that I was who I said I was. Thank God David was at the orphanage and wasn't even at work! But I also needed to get some proof for her. And I didn't know what that would be. I realized I could call the station and that she could ask one of the police who I was, at least. Maybe David would never find out.

I started praying hard.

"Can I at least explain what's going on? And you're free to call his office. I'll give you his number, but he's in Chicago right now at a conference. Please call and see that I'm telling the truth."

I handed her his card with the number on it. She called the desk at the St. Louis Police Station and asked to speak with Officer David Kelly.

I couldn't hear the conversation on the other side, but I heard her remark, "Oh, I see. No, I don't think anyone else can help. I'll call him when he gets back. Thank you."

She put the phone down.

"Well, you're correct about him not being in the office, and they say he's going to be in Chicago for a conference. But that still doesn't explain who you are. I'll give you five minutes to explain your so-called theory, but no more."

I thanked God quickly that she hadn't talked to anyone else at the station. The call would never get back to David. I took a deep breath and went on. "Sister Mary Patrick, or Sister Carolyn after she changed her name, wrote a book when she was teaching at St. Boniface. I was practice teaching there last year and only knew her by her former name. She came up to me one day and asked me to read her book. I think it was because I have a degree in English from Washington University, and I had left the convent after a year. Anyway, she told me the book was about meditation."

Mother Hannah looked skeptical. "I never heard about any book. And she was in our order. I'm sure she would have shared that book with us first."

"No, she wouldn't have. She gave me one of only two manuscripts she had. I wasn't excited about reading a book on meditation, but as soon as I got to the second page, I realized it wasn't about meditation at all."

"I don't understand. You said it was about meditation. What was it about?"

"It was a pretty steamy romance about a nun and a priest. It was very explicit. She wanted to get it published, make some money, and then leave the order. This was her ticket out. Then she got transferred, and I never heard from her again. A week ago, I was walking through a bookstore and saw a book with the same pen name we had thought up and the title, *Defiant Love*, so I bought it. It was her book, word for word."

"What? How could that possibly happen?"

"I have it right here with me."

I reached into my bag, pulled out the book and the manuscript, and handed them to Sister Hannah.

"You don't have to read much of it, just the first few pages, and you'll see they're almost exactly the same."

"I'll read whatever I want to read," she answered stubbornly.

I gave her a few minutes to look over the manuscript and the book. Her face went from puzzlement to anger. She put the book down and looked up at me.

I kept talking while I still had the chance.

"I think someone killed her, went through her belongings, found her manuscript, and got it published or finished the publishing process she'd started, and is collecting the money from the book. And it has to be someone in the convent. I want to go there for a few days and see what I can find out. Please let me. There's a life at stake here. We don't think Ramon, the vineyard master, killed her."

Mother Hannah sat very quietly for a few minutes. She kept looking at the book, and then back at the manuscript. I waited. I could have said more, but I was tired of explaining, and I wasn't sure it would do any good. So I gazed out the window to the buildings next door.

After what seemed like forever, she spoke. "I can't believe that this happened in my order. I know each one of these sisters personally, or I thought I did, but I will give you permission to go to Defiance and stay there for three days. I'll back up a story that you are undergoing some kind of treatment for a medical condition and need to rest. There's another problem you might not have considered though.

"What is that?" I thought I had everything figured out.

"Our congregation is very small, and we all know each other. It would be very suspicious if you went to Defiance as a member of our order. I think you should go there to rest and recover, but be from a different order here in the state. I'm thinking of the order of the Sisters called the Servants of Mary. They have a habit very similar to ours and none of our sisters would know the difference. I'll say they approached me because we have a secluded area where you could rest for a few days."

"That would be perfect, Sister. I appreciate your help."

"You do not have my permission to disrupt anyone's life or accuse anyone of murder. I don't know what you think you're going to find out that the police haven't already discovered, but if you think you can save someone from undeserved life in prison, then do whatever you can to find the truth. Three days is all you have. No more."

"Mother Hannah, I wish I didn't have to go there and do what I'm going to do, but I feel very strongly that this man Ramon didn't kill her, and my fiancé and I only want to find out the truth. I promise I won't accuse anyone, and if I don't find anything out in three days, I'll be gone and never bother anyone again. I appreciate you letting me do this."

"I would never allow it if a life weren't at stake."

"I'm as anxious to find out the truth as you are. Thank you."

"I'll make sure you have a habit so you'll fit in. When do you want to go there?"

"I'd like to go on Sunday afternoon, if that's all right."

"And you and your policeman friend believe this is the only way to find out who the murderer is?"

I hated to lie, but I had to. I didn't want Ramon to spend the rest of his life in jail for a murder he didn't commit. If I didn't find anything out, no one would be hurt, and David would never even know I had gone to Defiance. I couldn't think of anything that could go wrong with my plan.

Well, that wasn't true, either. There was probably a lot that could go wrong. I just couldn't think of anything specific at the moment.

So I lied. "Yes, we're hoping this will help with the investigation."

"I'll let Sister Gloria know that you'll be arriving, but not why. Just that you need to rest."

"Thank you. You have no idea what this might mean."

"I'll call a sister who will give you some clothes. All the new habits are very much the same. Blue skirt, white blouse, blue veil. I have a cross here that you can wear that's different from ours." She opened her desk drawer and took out a wooden cross on a chain I could wear.

She picked up the phone on her desk and talked to another sister.

"They'll have the habit for you. You can wait outside my office."

I got up and left the room. I sat in the comfortable chair in the outer office until a nun came with some clothes for me. She looked at me strangely, but handed me the clothes. I said thank you, turned, and left.

I put them in the trunk of my car in a bag from the grocery store. David would never look in there. Besides, he was getting ready for his trip, and we'd be taking his car to the airport.

CHAPTER 10

We woke up early Sunday morning so I could take David to the airport. It was a short flight to Chicago from St. Louis, but better than the six- or seven-hour drive to the conference.

We arrived at the terminal in plenty of time. I loved to see and hear the 707's taking off and landing at the airport. Such powerful engines. I hoped I could someday fly in one of those powerful jets. Maybe if we went somewhere exotic for our honeymoon, but we hadn't even talked about that yet.

I was thrilled that I'd gotten my Steinway piano instead of a large wedding and reception. Besides, I had never dreamed of a wedding like other girls did—some of them talked about that constantly. It sounded like they didn't care who they married as long as they got married. I think entering the convent was a bit of a rebellion against that attitude, although it didn't work out like I had hoped, since I had gotten thrown out.

I kissed David goodbye. He would be gone for almost a week, and although I had promised him I would never deceive him and always be honest with him, I knew he wouldn't approve of my latest scheme. I had to prove that Ramon wasn't the murderer, and I couldn't think of any other way to do it.

I drove home from the airport, packed a small suitcase—my old convent one—dressed in the clothes Mother Hannah had provided, put the cross around my neck, and got in the car for the drive to Defiance. It felt horrible to be in a habit again. I had gotten used to the freedom of dressing the way I wanted. I loved having the wind in my hair, and wearing jeans when I wanted to, and having to tuck my hair in a veil again and wear nylons and a skirt was frustrating. But I had to do this.

I had taken that one class in criminal justice at Washington University a few semesters ago, and I remembered a few things. I would have to get a search warrant to go through the sister's belongings. But David didn't need to have any of this as evidence he could use at a trial. If I could get some clues as to who might have committed the murder, that would help him. Then he could go and find the rest of the evidence he needed for the trial. I would only be finding a few leads for him.

The sisters, having been alerted that I was coming, greeted me warmly. If only they knew. I was sure I was given Sister Carolyn's old room, which had been thoroughly cleaned and redone. I wouldn't find anything there of any use.

Sister Henrietta helped me get settled and seemed very concerned about my health. She was a big, muscular woman. She was the housekeeper now, and it appeared she'd have no trouble doing all the household chores. We sat and talked for a while.

"You know, this was Sister Carolyn's old room," she mentioned.

"Oh?" I replied innocently. "She was the one who was murdered last year?"

"Yes, it was terrible. She hadn't come home for Vespers before dinner, and no one saw her all evening. Then late that evening, Ramon, the foreman, came to the door saying she had been murdered. It was obvious it had to be him."

"Why? He reported the murder. If he had killed her, why would he report the murder?"

"To try to shift the suspicion away from him, I guess. But all of us were here all evening, so it couldn't have been one of us, and Sister Carolyn was having an affair with him. That's why he killed her."

"Wow, how do you know she was having an affair with him?"

"She was always out in the vineyard and down at his house. It was obvious. Everybody knew about it."

"That's terrible." I didn't want to say anything else. But I asked, "Is walking in the vineyard safe?"

"Oh, yes. It was only dangerous then because of Ramon and because they were having an affair. It's perfectly safe to walk there now. All of us walk there. It's beautiful."

"Okay, that's good to know."

"Well, I'll let you get settled. Dinner is at six. See you there. The refectory is just down this hall and to the right."

"Thanks, Sister."

I unpacked a few things, even though I had no intention of staying any longer than I had to.

At six, I wandered down to the refectory and joined the other nuns. It felt so strange. I missed David a lot.

All the talk was about who was going where for the week. A few of the nuns were going on retreat. Sister Martin and Sister Angeline were going, but Sister Gloria and Sister Henrietta were staying at the convent. Sister Angeline had a cat, so she couldn't lock her door, but wanted to let Fuzzy the cat roam freely through the house, so it would be easier for me to get into her room. I hadn't figured out any of the details yet of how I would investigate this murder. My plan was just to see what happened. And David wouldn't even know I had come out here, especially if I didn't find anything. If I did find something, he would be thrilled that I had found the murderer.

The nuns sat around after dinner and watched TV, but I went to my room and read a book. I wasn't the slightest bit interested in "nun" talk anymore. I went to bed early. The next morning, we had breakfast at 6 a.m. and ate quickly so the nuns could get to seven o'clock Mass at St. Bonaventure, about a mile away. I had a bagel with cream cheese and some coffee, but I begged off going to church, saying I hadn't slept well and was recovering from my illness. They all left in the two convent cars.

I had my first chance to sneak around the house. I thought I'd try to see who occupied each room first. If I got caught wandering around, that wouldn't be too terrible. I'd wait until tomorrow to go into the rooms and investigate. I walked down the hall. Luckily, each room had the sisters' names typed on paper and inserted into a wooden strip beside the door. I encountered Sister Angeline's cat, Fuzzy, who had long hair and was striped grey and white, and not very friendly. He growled when I approached, so I didn't even attempt to pet him, unlike our kitties, Alex and JC, who were the friendliest and sweetest cats in the world.

I went back to the refectory and had a second cup of coffee. When the nuns came back from Mass, I tried to appear interested in their day.

By noon, the retreat nuns had departed, including Sister Emma, who was going to visit her parents, leaving Sister Gloria, Sister Henrietta, and me with the house to ourselves. I found Sister Henrietta in the kitchen and informed her that I would be taking a walk in the orchard for a while before my afternoon nap.

Sister Henrietta liked to talk. She asked me about my anemia, which I told everyone I was suffering from, and how I was feeling.

I didn't want to talk about it, but she was persistent.

"My sister had anemia, and they thought for a while it was aplastic anemia, which, as you know, can be fatal, but she was okay. What are you taking for yours?"

Damn. I had no idea what I was taking for my fake anemia symptoms, and I had no idea what aplastic anemia was or if I should even know. I made a guess. "The doctor wanted me to take some iron supplements and get lots of rest."

"I think that's probably the best thing. And make sure your diet is rich in iron too. Plenty of red meat."

I wanted to get away quickly.

"I think I'm going to take that walk now, if you don't mind."

"Oh, I'm sorry. I didn't mean to keep you from your walk."

"No, not at all. I think it'll be relaxing to walk in the vineyard."

And I didn't want to say that I also didn't have any more information about my fake diagnosis and was afraid to say another word about it.

I walked out the back door, which led directly to the vineyard. It was beautiful. Walking slowly down the long rows of vines beginning to leaf out gave me such a feeling of peace. I tried to walk slowly and deliberately in case anyone was watching. I had always loved gardens, and hoped that someday David and I could buy a house with many acres to plant. I didn't have any idea what I would plant; I just felt it was in my blood. My grandfather and father, who had lived in Ireland, had their own farm and had raised many crops, even in the harsh climate with long winters and short summers. I would have to talk to David about that, wondering if he wanted the same thing as I did.

I walked for about a half an hour—slowly, since I was tired—and returned to the house, where I retreated to my room, supposedly to take a nap. Instead, I sat and read a book for an hour or so. I could hardly wait for tomorrow to start my investigation. I really wanted to find something—anything—that David could use.

⋆ ⋆ ⋆

The next morning, Sister Gloria and Sister Henrietta left in one car for Mass, and I went into Sister Gloria's room first. I felt like a thief. That's what I was, though I didn't want to steal anything—just information. I looked in her desk drawer; nothing. She had file cabinets next to her desk, filled with school papers and lesson plans; the first two drawers overflowed with those. The third drawer contained school-administration papers, teacher pay stubs, and all the things one would expect to find in a principal's office. The fourth drawer looked promising, but it only held old photographs of her family and personal items, like letters from her parents and grandparents.

I truly felt like an intruder. There was no manuscript, no checks, nothing to indicate a publisher's name or anything that could link her to anything belonging to Sister Carolyn.

I made sure everything was exactly as I had left it, even making sure the door was open exactly as I had found it. I returned to the refectory and had another cup of coffee and a bagel with butter as they returned from Mass.

Sister Gloria asked what I was going to do all day and I answered, "I'm going to rest, and maybe walk in the vineyard again. It was so beautiful and peaceful there yesterday."

"It is lovely, and we shouldn't be having any rain for the next week or so. Well, enjoy the day. I have lots of paperwork to catch up with."

I called David that evening from the convent phone, knowing he wouldn't be able to reach me at home. I told him I was spending time with my mom and dad, and we were going to go to Forest Park tomorrow so I would be hard to reach. I asked how the conference was going. We talked for only a few minutes since it was a long-distance call and I told him I didn't want to add to my parents' phone bill, which he understood.

"See you in a few days, love. You'll still pick me up at the airport?"

"Of course. I can hardly wait to see you. But it's nice seeing my parents too. Love you."

The next morning, I decided to check out Sister Angeline's room.

CHAPTER 11

I waited until the car drove away. I had at least forty-five min-utes, and it wouldn't take me nearly that long. Nuns' rooms didn't have very much in them. A bed, a desk, a typewriter, some sort of file cabinet for all their papers, a closet for their meager assortment of clothes. That was it.

Her room was open so Fuzzy could come in or out. The litter box needed changing, but I wasn't the one who was going to do that. I hoped someone would, for the kitty's sake. I started with her desk drawer. Nothing of any interest. She had a small two-drawer file cabinet in the corner, and I opened the top drawer.

School papers, lesson plans, all the stuff of teachers. But David would be meticulous, so I went through almost every paper before I moved to the second drawer.

More of the same. But in the back, I saw the manuscript. Carolyn's manuscript. I kept looking. There were envelopes from the post office box number. I opened one. It had a can-celed check in it for $658 with the name Tiffany Blue. I opened another from about six months later for $1,324.35. I kept looking. I had to get my camera, but it was in my room. I put everything back carefully, even though Sister Angeline wouldn't be back for the entire week. I still had to document all of this, and the two nuns would be back from Mass very soon. I went as fast as I could, then closed the file cabinet and walked out the door, down the corridor, and into the refectory where I made another cup of coffee for myself. I could barely drink it, but I sat down like I had been there for hours and started to read a copy of the *St. Louis Post-Dispatch* from that morning.

Sister Angeline was the murderer. Now all I had to do the next morning was to take pictures of what I had found so I could show David. This had to be enough evidence to convince David that Sister Angeline was the murderer and save Ramon from being convicted of a murder he didn't commit.

I had a feeling David wouldn't be able to use any of the "evidence" in court, because I didn't have a search warrant or anything like that, but I had discovered who had really killed Sister Carolyn, and that was the information he needed. I had ruled out all the other nuns, and now he could get search warrants and the evidence correctly.

Sister Gloria came into the refectory. "How are you feeling today?" she asked politely.

"I'm okay. Still tired. I'll be staying with my parents for a few weeks. I just had to wait until they fixed up a room for me. I might even go tomorrow. But I really appreciate your offer to let me stay here to rest."

"I hope you'll get better soon. You're always welcome to stay here, you know. I'm sorry not all of us are here this week. It must be terribly boring around here."

"Not at all. I love going out in the vineyard and walking. It's a beautiful place you have here."

"We love it. Well, you do whatever you think is best for you."

"Thank you. I'll let you know."

I slept fitfully, thinking about how Sister Angeline had killed Sister Mary Patrick. I couldn't get her new name into my head. I'd known her as Mary Patrick and that would never change. She had published the book and would have made a profit from it. Now I knew where the profits were going and who was making the money.

As soon as the two sisters left for Mass the next morning, I took my camera and went back in Sister Angeline's room. I laid out all the material on her desk and took pictures with my camera. I only had one roll of film, so I had to be careful. I put everything back where I found it. I had enough for David to investigate.

When Sisters Gloria and Henrietta returned from Mass, I told them I had talked to my parents and would be leaving in an hour or so. I went to my room and packed my few belongings. With a simple goodbye, I got in my car and headed home.

David wouldn't be home for another few days, so I had plenty of time to relax at home with the kitties and still visit my parents. I pulled up, parked in the garage, turned the key in the door, and walked inside. David was sitting on the couch with his foot in a soft cast. He said hi, then looked at me strangely.

"What are you doing here? You're supposed to be at that conference." I was so surprised.

"Why are you dressed like that?" He sounded equally shocked.

I didn't answer.

"I was at the conference, and a few of us went out for a drink after the last meeting in the evening. We were walking back to the hotel, but one of the guys had way too much to drink and practically fell over on me. I tried to keep him from falling, but I slipped and sprained my ankle badly. The guys helped me into the hotel and we put ice on it. I went to the ER the next morning, but it isn't broken. It just hurts like hell, so I decided to just come home. I had already given my presentation the first day, so I didn't really need to be there for anything else. I tried calling you so many times, and I tried calling your parents, but they hadn't even seen you. So what's going on?"

I was caught for sure, but I had found out who had killed Sister Mary Patrick, so David would understand. He would more than understand. He'd be thrilled.

"Okay, when you went to Chicago, I decided to go out to the convent in Defiance and see what I could find out that might save Ramon and prove that he didn't kill Sister Mary Patrick. I had to do something."

David started frowning the moment I started talking. That wasn't a good sign. But I had to keep going.

"I talked to Mother Hannah, the superior of their order, and explained what I wanted to do, and she told the nuns there that I had been anemic and was going to stay there for a few days to rest and relax. So after I took you to the airport, I drove out there. I hoped I could find something to prove who was the real murderer—and David, I did! I found out Sister Angeline was the one who must have killed her. She has the manuscript for the book, and she's been collecting the money that the publisher has been sending to the P.O. box in Defiance. I don't know what she's been doing with the money, but she's been cashing the checks. I guess she's been depositing the money in her own account somewhere. So now you can use all that as evidence to show that Ramon didn't murder Sister Mary Patrick."

David looked angrier and angrier the more I talked. I thought for sure he would be thrilled that I had found out who the real murderer was.

"So it's your word against hers?" he finally asked.

"No, I took pictures of everything in her room. I have them all on my camera, but I haven't had time to develop the pictures yet. I just came back from there. That's why I'm still wearing their habit. I had no idea you were going to be here."

"You went into her room and looked through her belongings, and took pictures of them?"

"Yes, I did. I know that wasn't the right thing to do, and you probably can't use the pictures as evidence, but now you know it wasn't Ramon!"

"You went into people's rooms and searched them, without a warrant. And you're not a policeman. Nothing you have can be used as evidence. It was all illegally obtained. It's worse than useless. You could—you *should* be arrested for what you did!"

I thought he would at least be pleased that I had discovered who had committed the crime. "But now you know that Sister Angeline killed Sister Mary Patrick. You can investigate that on your own, even if you can't use my stuff."

"Also, you lied to me—again. That's the thing that bothers me more than anything. We said that we were going to be completely honest with each other. What you did was a complete and total lie. And it was premeditated, as well. I can't let that go. I've always tried to be honest with you, especially since we talked about honesty. Didn't that mean anything to you?"

I tried to explain. "Yes, of course it did, but I thought saving a man from jail for his whole life was more important than one little lie."

"It wasn't one little lie, and you know it. I don't think this is going to work for us anymore, is it?"

"What do you mean?" I got a sick feeling in my stomach.

"I don't feel like I can trust you anymore," he said simply.

David tried to move his leg from the chair to the floor.

"Does it hurt a lot?" I started to get up to help him, but he waved me away.

"No, it's not too bad. I took a few Tylenol before you came home. But we really need to talk about this."

David spoke quietly. He always did that when he was angry, which I luckily hadn't experienced very often.

"The thing that upsets me even more than knowing who might have killed Sister Carolyn and not being able to use the evidence is that you lied to me. We had that talk a few months ago about being completely honest with each other. I thought you meant it. I did. And this was a horrible lie. You lied about where you were, what you were doing, where you were going, everything. When I needed to get hold of you, I couldn't. But it's the lying that I can't live with."

I sat there silently. He was right. But I had to defend myself.

"Yes, I lied to you, and I'm sorry. But I did it so I could find out who really killed Sister Mary Patrick. The trial is coming up, and I had to do something."

He shook his head. "That's a great excuse, but it doesn't justify lying to me. I thought we were in this together. Now I know we're not."

"I won't do it again. I promise."

"You said that the last time. And the time before that." He turned and looked out the window. "You have no idea how many lies I hear every day. From suspects who are accused of crimes and have a million excuses and lie about everything to get out of it. I'm sick of it. And then to have the same thing at home? I don't think this is going to work."

I sat silently as tears streamed down my face. What had I done? I kept making the same mistake. I had the best intentions, or so I believed. Yet my impulsiveness and foolishness got in the way.

"And there's that other thing about having children. I want to have kids, and you don't, and we've never really settled that. I don't want you to have a child just because I want one. That's a huge commitment, and it's something you have to want, not just me. You and I will have to raise him or her together. So lying isn't the only reason this isn't going to work."

I had to explain my reasoning. "I don't want to spend eighteen or more years of my life—a whole lifetime, really—raising a child and being responsible for someone else. I'm not ready for that. But I might be at some point. I don't know, and I don't want to say I will be if I'm not sure."

I didn't know what else to say, but I knew it had better be the truth. "Do you need anything before I go to bed? I'm going to sleep in the guest bedroom," I managed to say without crying.

"No, I'm fine. I think that would be the best thing. We can talk in the morning about what we're going to do."

I got up, walked into the master bedroom, collected all my things for the night, and went to the guest bedroom. I said goodnight. David only nodded. He was petting the cats who were sitting on his lap and off to his side. I closed the door and sat on the bed. He had broken up with me, I realized suddenly, and the tears came. I couldn't hold them back anymore.

How could I have been that idiotic? All that planning, and going into the nuns' rooms, and discovering the murderer's identity, and taking the pictures—all of it was a stupid, stupid idea. And now it was the end of the only relationship I had ever had. With the only person I had ever loved. And it was all my fault.

I always did things like this. Impulsive and childish. I had good motives, but things turned out badly. I had gotten kicked out of the convent because of my impulsive behavior. I was lucky that turned out as well as it did.

And finding the *Silent Night* manuscript was just pure luck. I should have never gone to Franklin to be around that murder investigation. There were so many times I had acted naively and impulsively, but this was the worst one, and now I had ruined my whole life because of it.

David was right. I couldn't be trusted. I had shown him too many times that I couldn't be trusted. Oh, I had excuses for all my behavior. Valid and good excuses, worthwhile reasons, but the bottom line was that he couldn't trust me. And I was responsible for that. He had repeatedly warned me, but I always ignored his warnings. And now it was too late.

I got dressed in my nightgown and crawled into bed, hugging the pillow tightly. It was no substitute for his warmth. I didn't know what I'd do in the morning. This was his apartment; I'd given mine up last year. I'd leave. I'd go to my parents' for a few weeks. But I couldn't bear their questions about what had happened between David and me. Maybe I could stay with Pam. No, she only had a one-bedroom apartment, so I couldn't impose on her.

Maybe David and I could settle this in the morning. I started crying again. No, we couldn't. This was too serious. This was a fundamental problem that had ruined our relationship. I missed him. I already missed his warmth, his kisses, everything about him. What had I done? I tried to talk myself out of it, but I had done many things that were wrong. David hadn't done anything wrong. Oh, he wasn't perfect. He could be bossy and opinionated, and he thought he was right about most things. He often acted like a policeman when he got home at night, and I had to remind him that he wasn't at work anymore. He apologized when he acted like that, because I told him when it was happening, and we usually laughed about it afterwards. But he was almost always kind, loving, appreciative, and honest.

I cried until I couldn't cry anymore. I sat up, wrapped the blanket around me, and watched the river and the tugboats floating up and down with their lights flickering as they passed the trees on the shore. I wondered if David was asleep in the next room. I finally lay down and fell asleep.

CHAPTER 12

When I woke up, I got up right away and went to the kitchen, hoping David was still there and that everything would be back to normal. He was at the kitchen table reading the paper.

"How are you feeling?" I asked him.

"I feel okay. How about you?" he asked a little too politely.

"I didn't sleep very well," I said honestly.

"Me neither."

I poured myself some coffee and sat down with him. I decided to be the first to say something.

"Maybe I could stay with my parents for a while."

I was hoping he would say no.

He didn't look at me, but looked beyond me, out the window. "That might be the best thing."

I sat quietly, unsure of what to say next. I desperately wanted him to say something—anything.

"Are you staying home today?" I asked.

"I'm taking a few days off, to rest."

"I'll call my parents this morning."

"Okay."

I couldn't sit there any longer. I got up, went into our bedroom, and got dressed. By the time I came back out, David was back to reading the paper and didn't look up at me. I didn't feel like eating, so I went back into the bedroom and packed a few clothes. How long would I be gone? Was this going to be forever, or a week, or a month? I had no idea. Was it the end? I didn't want it to be, but we both had to take some time off.

★ ★ ★

Walking into my parents' house was one of the most difficult things I ever had to do. I was going to tell them I was there for only a week and that David had gone to a conference, but I realized that would be another lie, and I couldn't do that. I had to tell them the truth, no matter how much it hurt.

"Kristen, you said you were coming for the week? It's so good to see you. Is everything okay?" Mom said as she opened the screen door for me. As soon as I looked at her, I burst into tears.

"Honey, what's wrong?" She hugged me, which was very unusual for my family. "Are you okay? Is David okay?"

"We're fine," I sobbed. "We broke up, and I don't know if we'll ever get back together."

"Oh, no. Put the suitcase down and come into the kitchen and sit down."

I followed her and sat down at the old, gray-speckled Formica table, where I told her the whole story.

When I finished, she tried to be encouraging. She poured me a drink of Dr. Pepper and got one for herself.

"Don't give up, honey. Every couple goes through this. If you love each other, you'll make it. He'll realize how much he loves you, and you'll get back together."

I couldn't stop crying. "It's not that simple, Mom."

"I know it isn't, but I still think you two are meant for each other."

We talked a little longer, and she really made me feel better. Just talking to her and having someone understand was a big help, even if it didn't solve anything. I helped around the house and decided to go shopping at the mall in the afternoon. I bought some much-needed new clothes for school and a few comfortable shoes, and by the time I got home, Dad was there. Mom had explained everything and had prepared a great pasta meal, so we sat at the table and talked about the neighbors, a safe subject.

I went into my old room, carefully preserved. I heard the phone ring, and my heart stopped. Maybe it was David. But I heard my mom say hi to Joann, and then I couldn't hear the rest of the conversation. He didn't call that evening, or the next. I read books for my classes in the fall and reluctantly created a few lesson plans. I didn't want to call him, but my heart was empty.

Sooner or later, I'd have to decide whether to rent an apartment. I couldn't live with my parents for too long. It was only the second night. He had to call in a day or two. I went to sleep after I cried all the tears I could possibly cry.

After the fourth day, I went to my old bedroom early while my parents watched TV. I changed into my pajamas and went to bed, but I couldn't sleep. I got up and sat at my old roll top desk. I used to do my homework there every night when I was in high school, hoping to get accepted to a good college. Mom hadn't cleaned out the desk, but kept everything the way it was when I left, hoping? There were little treasures I had collected—a rainbow colored Murano paperweight from Italy, an old fabric doll from when I was much younger,

I sat at the desk and realized that I should call David. Why was I waiting for him to call? I was the one who had lied and had caused the problem. I should be the one calling and asking to talk. I was an adult, but I was acting like a teenager waiting for her boyfriend to call. Does he like me? Will he call and ask for a date? Did he notice me today in class? I was being ridiculous. I was an adult in a real relationship—we were about to get married!

But I realized I didn't know what to say if he answered the phone. I had made a terrible mistake by lying. But I did it for the right reasons. And he would never have agreed to the plan if I had told him. But David should understand that my actions, short-sighted as they were—might be the thing that saved Ramon from spending his life in jail for a crime he didn't commit! And we would have never found out who the real killer was if it hadn't been for me.

I was so tired. From thinking, from crying, from not knowing what to do. I got up and slipped back into bed. I would call first thing in the morning.

When I woke up the next morning, I waited until David was probably up. I pulled the phone into my bedroom. It rang and rang, but he didn't answer. He had probably left for work. My mom fixed oatmeal with cinnamon and raisins, with a cup of hot chocolate. I went back in the bedroom and called his station.

"Hello, could I speak to Officer David Kelly?"

"I'm sorry, he's out of the office right now. Can someone else help you?"

"No, thank you." I put the phone down. Maybe the trial had started. He would have to be there, at least for the beginning, and for his testimony. Or maybe they were still choosing the jury. I'd call later.

I called our apartment that evening, but no answer. He didn't call for the next few days. And every night our phone rang. Sometimes two or three times, before my mom got up from the living room and made her way out to the kitchen and picked it up. Each time, my heart started to beat quickly, but it was never David.

Six days went by.

Even though the trial might have started, he could have called in the evening. I called him, but couldn't reach him. Every day I cried, but every day got a little easier. I started wondering what my life would be like now that I was by myself again. The first few nights were frightening, and the future looked bleak. But as the days went by and he didn't call, I began to get angry at him for not even bothering to call me, and that helped.

If his love for me wasn't good enough for us to sit down and talk about the argument—if he didn't even call to let me know whether I should pack up my things and figure out where I'd be living—the angrier I got. He had problems too, and I wasn't the only one at fault.

I still loved him, but people who cared for each other discussed their problems, and we weren't doing that. My sadness and tears turned into frustration and stubbornness.

Oh, I still missed him, and I wanted to be with him, but I began to realize he wasn't perfect either. Maybe we weren't meant for each other. Maybe it took more than love to make a relationship work. Maybe we didn't have what it took.

I sat down with my mom that evening and talked to her about it.

"Mom, David hasn't called, and it's been six days. I've called him a lot, but I can't reach him. The trial's probably started, and I know he's busy, but he isn't even home in the evenings. I think it's over. I'm kind of angry that he hasn't called."

"I would be, too. You have to find out what's going to happen with all your things. You're welcome to stay here for as long as you want. You know that."

"Thanks, Mom, but I'll probably get my own place. This is too far from where I teach."

"I understand. You don't need a forty-five-minute drive each way into school. But if there's anything we can do—"

"Oh, no, you've already done so much. I really appreciate it."

CHAPTER 13

David went to work the morning Kristen left for her parents.' He was in a terrible mood. He hadn't slept all night, tossing and turning. He missed her already, but they had to talk about this. He sat at his desk with a cup of coffee, milk and a packet of sugar. He stirred it absentmindedly. George Hoffman walked by his desk. "You know, if you just keep stirring it and not drinking it, it's going to get cold."

David looked up at him, then down at his coffee. "Oh, yeah, right."

"You working on something important?"

"I'm trying to. I don't know what to do first."

"Well, finish your coffee. You look like you've been up all night."

"I have. I need to figure out some things."

"Can I help you with anything?"

"I wish you could, but I don't think so."

"Well, let me know if you need anything."

"Thanks."

David took a sip of coffee. It was still too hot.

He decided to call the old convent where Sister Carolyn had been stationed with Kristen and talk to the superior there. He didn't even know the name of the superior. He found the number, called and made an appointment with Sister Rosemary that morning. It wasn't a long drive. He'd made it plenty of times, following Kristen last year when her life was in danger.

He knocked on the door and went inside with a sister he had never seen before. She asked him to wait in the parlor, but Sister Rosemary came out quickly and brought him to her office.

"Sister, I'm just asking a few questions about Sister Carolyn. You knew her as Sister Mary Patrick when she was stationed here last year."

Sister Rosemary looked down. "It was so terrible what happened to her. That man who killed her? I hope he goes to jail for the rest of his life. He killed a wonderful, kind person who cared about people."

"Yes, my fiancée is Kristen Byrne. She practice taught here last year, and met Sister Mary Patrick. She told me all about her."

"And you're investigating the case? That's wonderful. To have someone who cares and knows the victim personally. That must make a real difference in the investigation." "Well, I didn't know her personally, but Kristen told me a lot about her, and I agree, the person who killed her needs to be brought to justice." David went on, "Did you know that Sister Mary Patrick was writing a book?"

"No, I had no idea." She sat quietly for a few seconds. "Was it published already?"

"Yes, it was published the summer before she got transferred."

"That explains a lot."

"What do you mean?" David was confused.

"Well, I got a letter from a publisher in New York a few months ago addressed to Sister Mary Patrick. I opened it because she was deceased, and there was no one to forward it to, and it showed her earnings from last year. It was a tax form. The earnings came to over three thousand dollars! I didn't know what to do with the information. We don't pay taxes since we're a charitable institution and we're exempt. She was dead, God rest her soul, so I put the letter in my files and didn't do anything with it. I didn't know what I could do about it anyway."

"Can I see the letter, Sister?"

"Of course. Let me find it."

She got up and went to the file cabinet in the corner of the room. She opened the third drawer, looked through some files, found the letter, walked back, and handed it to David.

David took it and looked at the envelope. "It's addressed to Sister Mary Patrick. I guess she hadn't changed her name yet when she signed the contracts with the publishing company."

Sister Rosemary was shocked. "She made all that money from a book? And we had no idea? I find that hard to believe. How can I get a copy of it? Was it a religious book? I'm amazed that a book about religion would sell so well in this day and age."

David wasn't about to discuss the book at this time, so he just said, "I'll try to get a copy of it for you, Sister," knowing he was lying. But he didn't know what else to say.

He had more important things to think about right now, like where all the money went once Sister Angeline got hold of it.

"I'm sorry I kept that letter, Officer, I didn't know what to do with it, especially since she had passed away and we don't pay taxes anyway."

"I'll keep it for now. We might need it for evidence in the trial."

"Oh, of course. I had no idea it would be important."

He had to get another search warrant to go to the post office in Defiance. He could do that in the morning, or maybe this afternoon, if he was quick. He thanked Sister Rosemary for her help and took his leave.

He drove to the courthouse again. He knew the judge was getting tired of him, but it was easy to get another search warrant after he had explained the situation. He got a warrant for the bank in Defiance also, assuming there was only one bank there. He doubted if there were two in such a small town. He called the convent to make sure the sisters would be there this afternoon and discovered that they all would be. It was already one o'clock in the afternoon when he started out, with Sister Carolyn's book on the front seat next to him.

He was still angry at Kristen for lying to him, but realized that without her stupid actions of last week, Ramon would probably be found guilty at the trial next week. David had to act fast. She had done what she had done in a sincere attempt to discover the truth, and it was more than he had found out in six months of investigation.

He took a Dr. Pepper in the car with him since it was a long ride, and an hour later, he pulled up to the familiar parking lot by the convent that overlooked the vineyard. It was beautiful out here, especially in summer, with the green vines spreading everywhere for acres. The last time he had been here was in November of last year, and it had been cold and dead.

He grabbed the book, got out of the car, and walked up to the old wooden door, where he rang the doorbell. Sister Gloria answered. They knew each other well by this time. "Come in, come in. Do you want something to drink after your long drive?"

"Water would be just fine, Sister."

Sister Gloria returned quickly with a glass of water.

"I had a few more questions for you, Sister."

"Oh, I thought we had been over everything about what happened to Sister Carolyn."

"Did you know anything about a book that Sister Carolyn wrote?"

"A book? No, she never wrote a book. We would certainly have heard about it if she had written one."

"You never saw any evidence that she was writing one? A manuscript, letters to and from a publisher, anything like that?"

"No, like I said, we would have known."

David handed her the book. "This is her book."

Sister Gloria glanced at the cover with the risqué picture of a man and woman embracing.

"This isn't a book by Sister Carolyn! It doesn't even have her name on it. And she would never write anything like this trash!"

David tried to explain, "When my fiancée, Kristen, was teaching at St. Boniface, she met Sister Carolyn, Sister Mary Patrick at the time, and Sister gave her a copy of a manuscript. They came up with this pen name together one day while discussing the manuscript. Kristen lost track of her over the summer but learned what happened to Sister Carolyn, and she also found the book at the bookstore a week ago. It's Sister Carolyn's book, word for word."

Sister Gloria sat perfectly still, holding the copy of the book. "I can hardly believe it. I had no idea. How did she think she could publish something like this and stay in our order?"

"Kristen told me that Sister Carolyn was planning on leaving as soon as she made enough money from the book sales. You've never received any money for her, have you?"

"No, this is the first I've even heard about it. I still can't believe it. But you say it's the same as the manuscript she gave your fiancée?"

"Yes, the same."

"Do you want me to call the other sisters and ask them if they knew anything about this?"

"Yes, if you could do that."

Sister Gloria got up and turned to David. "We're going to be in the chapel for prayers in a few minutes. I'll tell the sisters to come in here after prayers. It should only be about fifteen minutes."

"That's fine. I'll wait."

Sister Gloria seemed sincere, David thought. This would give him a good chance to see Sister Angeline and how she acted when she was told about the book. David hoped he was getting better at reading people, but wasn't too sure how gifted he was in that area.

He waited for about twenty minutes before the sisters came into the parlor. They greeted him tentatively, each one sitting down quietly and waiting until they all had gathered.

David told them what he had told Sister Gloria about the book and watched their reactions carefully. Most of them looked surprised. One of the sisters said, "She spent a lot of time in her room by herself, even during recreation. We thought she was shy. I guess she was writing."

"She had already finished the book, and it was in the process of being published when she was killed," David said. "She might have been working on something else, though."

A few of the sisters nodded. Sister Angeline managed to look as surprised as the other four sisters, and David couldn't detect anything from her facial expression.

"We didn't find any evidence at all in her room after she was killed that she had even written a book."

One of the sisters, Sister Martin, said, "That seems strange. What do you think she did with it? And what kind of book did she write? Do you know?"

"Yes, I have it right here." He took out of his briefcase and passed it to the first nun. She looked at the title and the cover art and her face turned red. "I can't believe she wrote this."

She quickly passed it on to Sister Emma, who looked up at David. "How did she think she was going to get away with this?"

David said simply, "Well, she did. And she got it published—that's her pen name, of course."

Sister Martin asked, "Are you absolutely sure this is her book?"

"Yes. My fiancée, Kristen, has her original manuscript, and it's the same, word for word, as this book. Someone's been collecting her royalties and cashing them. Someone who knew about the book."

Sister Emma was the talkative one. "And none of us here knew anything about it. Is that why you came back here? To question us about the book and see if anyone knew anything?"

"Yes, that's one of the reasons. Also, there might be some information we might have missed during our first investigation. If you have anything, please feel free to tell me about it. Ramon's trial starts next week, and this will be the last time we can get any evidence to use in court."

"I wish we could help you more," Sister Gloria said sincerely.

David noticed that Sister Angeline had been the quietest of all the sisters. He knew why, even though no one else did. And she certainly wasn't going to volunteer any information willingly. Her face was serene and placid during the whole conversation.

David thanked the sisters for their time and told them he would let them know what happened at the trial, since it involved people they had known and cared for.

"I think it'll be a short trial, so you'll probably hear from me in the next few weeks."

He stood, and Sister Gloria and all the nuns stood and said goodbye to him.

CHAPTER 14

The drive home was long, and the traffic was terrible. He thought about Kristen the whole way. He needed to call her, but he had been so busy following up on the information she provided that he hadn't had the chance.

That was a lie. He did have the opportunity to call her. He just didn't know what to say. He'd call her tomorrow. He didn't have any trouble interviewing people or talking to large groups, but this was different. Too much was at stake. Over the last few days, he began to realize how unforgiving he had been in their last conversation when he accused her of lying to him. She had lied to him but did it for a good reason. Without her going to that convent and spying on those nuns, Ramon would be facing a possible life sentence for the murder of someone he hadn't killed. He still might, if David couldn't get the evidence he needed. Kristen had lied, but he had to forgive her.

He hoped they could work it out. They had to talk about this lying problem. David valued honesty above everything, and it bothered him that she wasn't honest with him about something so important. She was probably right, though. He would never have agreed to her going to Defiance and posing as a nun to gather information. They could have come up with something, though. He just couldn't imagine what it would have been. He hoped she hadn't given up on him. It had been days since they had argued, and he hadn't even called once to tell her to get her things or talk about how long she should stay with her parents.

He was exhausted when he got to St. Louis, so he stopped by the Italian restaurant and picked up a lasagna dinner.

By the time he ate dinner and fed the noisy cats, it was already ten thirty and too late to call. He'd call her tomorrow.

He got up early the next morning, went to the courthouse to get another search warrant, then made the long drive back to Defiance. There was only one bank in the town, a Bank of America in a shopping center a few miles away from the convent. Sister Angeline had to have set up an account there.

After he identified himself and showed his search warrant to the bank president, it was easy to locate an account under Sister Mary Patrick's name, and to see the deposits that were made in the months after her death.

Sister Angeline had obviously gone to the post office, gotten the checks, signed them in Sister Mary Patrick's name, and deposited each one in Sister Mary Patrick's account. She was probably waiting until she had enough money to leave, just like Sister Carolyn (Mary Patrick) would have done if she had lived.

David walked out of the bank and got into his car. Now he needed to get the actual bank statements and receipts from Sister Angeline. He would need another search warrant for that, and then he would have all the evidence he needed in his hands. He was running out of time, and hoped that he'd be able to introduce this new evidence at the trial. The prosecution might ask for a continuance, but he'd just have to hope that wouldn't happen.

Sister Angeline had no idea that anyone knew what she had done. She was probably confident that Ramon would be found guilty in the coming weeks. He was the only suspect.

David thought again about Kristen. It was Friday. Six days had passed since their argument. He should have called. He would call when he got home, even though he didn't know what to say. He missed her every second of every day and knew without a doubt that they had to repair their relationship.

CHAPTER 15

The next evening I was going to call him, but the phone rang after dinner. Mom got it and called me.

"It's for you," she said without any emotion.

I pulled the phone, cord and all, into my bedroom, and closed the door.

"Kristen, it's David. How are you?"

"I'm okay." Keep it neutral.

"Can you talk for a few minutes?"

"Of course."

"Listen, I'm really sorry about everything. Especially about not calling you for so long. Can we meet at our place tomorrow afternoon and talk?"

"I guess so. What time?"

"Let's pick up some lunch. Would that be okay?"

"Fine, I'll see you then."

"Okay, bye."

I hung up the phone and sat on the hardwood floor for a few minutes. What was that all about? Did he want to get back together? It didn't sound like it. He sounded friendly enough. But not loving. Not like he missed me and wanted me back in his life. I didn't know what to think. Okay, I wasn't going to think about it. I would just go tomorrow and see what would happen.

I thought about it anyway—all evening and all night and all the next morning. What was going to happen? What did I want?

Did I want to keep this relationship going? Did I have a choice? Was it over? Was it totally his decision? Was it mine? Was it mutual?

I was worn out just thinking about it. I went for a walk in the morning. It was a beautiful day. The clouds were a fluffy white and there was no rain in the forecast. The temperature was a comfortable seventy-five, a perfect June day. The heat would be back very soon, so I enjoyed this unexpectedly cool weather for as long as it would last.

I drove to "our" apartment around eleven thirty and knocked on the door. He didn't answer so I let myself in. The kitties were so glad to see me. I'd missed them so much. I would take JC with me wherever I went, and I would take my Steinway piano with me. David had no use for it. I guess marriage was out of the question now.

I fixed myself a Dr. Pepper from the refrigerator and sat on the couch. I didn't want to pack my things yet. We had to talk first. I heard David at the door.

"Hi, I'm sorry. I had to pick up some things at the store. I've been busy this week."

I stood up, unsure of what to do. I wanted to hug him and kiss him, but instead I just said "Hi, how are you? How's your sprained ankle?"

"It's getting better. I've been so busy at work. The trial starts next week. I have so much to tell you. Let me fix a drink first."

"Sure."

He went out in the kitchen and grabbed a drink.

"Have you eaten yet?"

"No."

"Do you think we can talk at a restaurant? If we get a booth away from everybody else? How about that little Greek restaurant? It should be pretty empty this time of day."

"Okay, I guess so." I wasn't sure if our talk would involve lots of tears, but I had cried all the tears I had inside me the past week, so I didn't know if I had any left anyway.

We walked down to his car and drove the two miles to the restaurant.

They led us to a table in the corner by a window and got our order for drinks.

I just got water.

No one was there except a family with about four kids across the room, and they certainly wouldn't be listening to anything we had to say.

David sat across from me. "First of all, I want to apologize for not calling you this week."

I looked down at the table. "I was really hurt by that. It would have only taken a second to call and let me know whether you wanted me to come back or talk or pick up my things or so many other things. But you didn't even bother."

David took my hand, and I let him.

"I'm really sorry. I did a lot of thinking those first few days, and then I started to investigate everything you had told me about Sister Angeline, and I got caught up in the investigation. I had to find something I could use in court. Thanks to you, we knew that Sister Angeline was the murderer, but I had to find the evidence on my own. I couldn't use yours."

"You could have made a quick phone call one of those days. I tried calling you so many times."

"I know, and I'm sorry I didn't. I hope you can forgive me for that. Let's talk about the lying and get that over with first."

I wasn't sure if I even wanted to talk about that. We'd been over it before.

"You already told me our relationship is over, that you can't be with someone you don't trust. Someone who lied to you. It's taken me a whole week to realize we'll never be together again, but I think it's probably for the best." I tried not to cry.

"Wait a minute. We need to talk. Can I say a few things?"

"Okay," I managed to whisper.

"I guess that honesty is something I value more than almost anything else in a relationship. I don't want us to ever have a lie ruin what we have together. But that being said, I also realized how unfair I've been to you this whole week. I thought I had such wonderful morals and was a great person, but I couldn't even forgive you for a lie you told in good faith to save someone's life. I started to feel terrible when I recognized that what I was doing was far worse than anything you'd ever done. If I can't forgive you, I lack kindness and goodness in my heart, and I don't want to be like that. It took me a while to realize this, though, because I was really angry with you. I thought you should have told me what you were going to do. But I would never have agreed to it. So you were right about that. And we would have never found out that Sister Angeline was the murderer. I've tried to think of how we could have come up with a plan that might have worked, but I sure can't think of one. So you were right about not telling me in that regard."

"I knew you would never have agreed to let me go to Defiance. You would have told me not to get involved. And I shouldn't have. It was way too risky. And illegal. And I'm sorry that I did it."

"But if you hadn't gone out there, Ramon would certainly have been convicted of murder, and that would be a terrible crime."

David went on, "So if you can, please accept my apology. I think we both have some things to work on in our relationship, but I believe we can make it work. I love you so much, and that must count for something."

I sat there, tears running down my face. I didn't care who saw me or what they thought of me. The waiter came up to the table.

He took one look at me and said, "I'm sorry. I'll come back"

David said, "No, that's fine. I'll order." He looked at me. "Is that okay?"

I nodded.

We got back to our talk as soon as the waiter walked away.

I understood it took a lot for David to apologize to me and to recognize what he had learned about himself.

"You're not the only one who learned something about themselves, David. I really will try to be completely honest with you in the future. No more excuses, no more lying to get what I think is a good result. We can talk about how to do things together in the future. I'm so sorry I deceived you. I promise it won't ever happen again."

"Do you think we could try again?" He reached across the table and took my hand again.

I had to say it. This was just too important.

"David, I can't wait six days to talk to you about any problems we're having. We have to talk about things right away, even if we're not sure what to say to each other. I don't ever want to live through another week wondering if we're going to be together or alone."

"I have no excuse for not calling you. I could blame it on my schedule or my parents and say they never talked about their conflicts or feelings, but those are excuses. I'm an adult, and I don't want to be like them at all. I promise you right now that I will always talk to you about problems between us, even if I'm not sure what to say."

"And I'll try to do the same. I want this to work. I missed you. I can make it on my own in this life, but I'd rather be with you."

"Okay, that's it, then. Let's eat. And then I have to get back to the courthouse. The trial starts in a day, but I don't think it should last too long. And then I'll have so much to tell you about it."

The waiter brought the chicken shish-ka-bab and hummus. The last thing I wanted to do was eat, but I ate the food anyway. And it tasted pretty good. I hadn't realized how hungry I was. I had to call Mom when I got home and tell her everything was okay.

Home. That was a great word—our home.

David and I got back to the apartment, and he left for the courthouse. I called my mom.

She was thrilled that we had worked everything out. I went back to my parents' house to pick up my things and then spent the rest of the afternoon with JC and Alex. I caught up on my practicing. I couldn't believe that a week away from the piano had taken such a toll on my playing. I practiced for two hours, until JC couldn't stand it a moment longer and let me know with his loud meows.

David was busy the whole week, even though his role at the trial was limited. His testimony was over on the second day, but he continued to be in the courtroom for the entire proceedings. He felt it was his duty to be there.

He breathed a sigh of relief when the jury left for the day and would be in the jury room the next day. He got the call midday and went to the courtroom to hear the verdict. It was a simple one. Sister Angeline was convicted of murder and received the maximum sentence. Ramon was a free man.

David came home looking happier than I had seen him in months.

"Okay, tell me everything you can about the trial," I said.

"I can tell you because it's all over now. Let's start at the beginning. Even though you obtained that information about

Sister Angeline illegally, it was sufficient to initiate my own investigation. I called the convent where Sister Mary Patrick had been stationed last year and spoke to the superior. She informed me they had received a tax form for Sister Mary Patrick from the publisher that they didn't know how to handle. She set it aside because Sister Mary Patrick was deceased. They never took any action with it and never reported it. So I obtained a search warrant for it and discovered how much money she had received from the publisher in the last six months before she died. The money had to be filed under her real name, not her pen name, for tax purposes. It was over three thousand dollars. And, of course, no one had any idea where the money had gone. So that was my next problem—to find out who had been taking the money."

"That was great luck. That she had that tax form, or whatever it was. I'll bet Sister Angeline didn't count on that."

"No, I'm sure she didn't. Then I went to Defiance and talked to the sisters there again. Sister Angeline just sat there and didn't give anything away. She looked as surprised as the rest of them when I mentioned the book that Sister Carolyn had written. With your help, I went to the judge and obtained a search warrant for the post office to try to discover who had been collecting the checks from the P.O. box there. As it turned out, at least one of the tellers knew Sister Angeline since she had taught a few of them in grade school, and could testify that she came once a month to pick up mail. She didn't have a box in her name."

"That was lucky that someone there knew her!"

"Yes, but it doesn't really prove anything. Then I obtained another warrant for the bank and discovered she had been depositing the money into Sister Mary Patrick's account all the months after she died. Now I had all the evidence I need for the trial, thanks to you. Without your illegal activity, we would never have known where to look. I certainly don't condone what you did, but I'm glad we were able to convict the right person."

"But you didn't have all the papers and everything that was in Sister Angeline's room at the convent?"

"Yes, I got another warrant for that and got everything you took pictures of, and it was all used as evidence for the trial. Ramon's lawyer was thrilled to have it and was able to introduce it at trial—with the judge's permission, of course. The defense might have asked for a continuance, but they didn't. And the evidence was so damning against Sister Angeline, I don't think the jury had much of a choice but to convict her. It only took them a few hours."

The kitties were still glad to see me, and fought over who would sit on my lap. It was easier when David was home, because he got one or the other. JC curled up on my lap, purring loudly.

"What are you thinking?" I was the one to ask David this time.

He sat beside me on the couch, gently holding my hand and playing with my fingers.

"I couldn't bear to separate the two cats. They've become such good friends by now. It would be so difficult for them to lose each other."

He leaned over and kissed me. A long, wonderful kiss.

I looked at him and smiled. "I totally agree. There are a lot of reasons we should be together, but the cats are the best reason."

David continued to hold my hand. "I don't want to break their little hearts. That would be such a terrible thing to do. I'm not sure they would ever recover."

"I don't think they ever would," I answered, and then we didn't talk anymore.

Author's Note

Old Habits Die Hard: Fact or Fiction?

Even though *Old Habits Die Hard* is fiction, many of its elements are based in fact.

First of all, no one was ever murdered in the motherhouse or in any convent. The crimes are all fictional. Most of the nuns I knew were kind and generous, though a few had a rather tyrannical approach to our training.

However, many other elements of the book are based on my real experiences during my six years as a nun with the School Sisters of Notre Dame in St. Louis.

The sisters' missions were typical of real missions in the 1960s.

I spent two years on a mission after leaving the motherhouse, during which I taught at a high school in central Missouri, similar to the one in the fictional city of Franklin.

I was fortunate to be at a large convent with over thirty sisters, but many people in my class were assigned to missions consisting of three nuns: the superior, an older nun, and the new arrival. It was a challenging adjustment to make.

Sister Anne, the musician and choir director in the first story called "Hot Chocolate," would have found it difficult to adjust to her new life in her small mission and might have felt very lonely. The lives of priests are also lonely, lacking the companionship that many of us have and often take for granted. While many find that their work and service to the Church compensate for this loneliness, others do not. It is estimated that between forty and fifty percent of priests who have taken a vow of celibacy have broken it. Unfortunately, the Catholic Church has never addressed this issue like many Protestant churches, which permit their clergy to marry and have families, and allow and encourage women to become ministers. The Catholic Church suffers from a severe shortage of priests, and addressing the celibacy and gender issue could help resolve the problem.

The second story in the book, "Revenge," revolves around the Marino family, a fictional family connected to the Mafia. While the entire family is made up, it draws from my understanding of the Mafia in St. Louis during the 1960s. My sister worked for a lawyer in St. Louis for many years; a man who became a good friend of our family. He even built tennis courts on his large estate so he could play tennis with my father, a Missouri State champion. Throughout my childhood and into my teenage years, we visited his home numerous times. Tragically, he was murdered by the Mafia in his fifties. His body was discovered washed up on a beach in Florida, riddled with bullet holes. It was then that we learned he had been affiliated with the Mafia, and many years later, we found out that he had been killed because he was going to testify against them in court. I used his personal background as inspiration for the lawyer in my story, highlighting his loyalty to his sister, Jeanette.

The wine industry thrived in Missouri during the 1960s, and many regions produce excellent grapes in their wineries. I used this as the backdrop for the final story, "The Vineyard," and featured a real city located in the Missouri wine country.

Just as in the first book, the sisters struggle with the rules of the orders, and many decide to leave, not only because life is difficult, but because many of the rules are meaningless and outdated. Even now, most of the roles of women in the church are not as significant as men's. Becoming a priest is a sacrament, but becoming a nun is not. I'm uncertain if women will ever achieve equality with men in the Catholic Church. I'm also not sure if women will ever be equal in our society, although we have made great strides compared to many other countries.

I mentioned the racial issues in "The Vineyard" regarding Kristen and Michael's friendship because they were an important aspect of life in the Midwest during the late sixties and early seventies. The Civil Rights Act was only passed in 1965, and although the law mandated no discrimination based on skin color or ethnicity, society often conveyed a different narrative. My friend Pam, who has been one of my closest friends for my entire life, shared many stories about her family's concerns regarding interracial dating and even friendships. Her parents worried each time her brothers went out in the evenings during high school and college, hoping they would return home safely.

I moved to California after leaving the convent and dated a Black student at UCLA. I felt quite comfortable dating him, but California was significantly more progressive than the Midwest at that time.

One of the facts of the late 1960s and '70s was the lack of telephone communication compared to today. I find it hard to believe that I could go an entire day, traveling for hours on a bus to school and back, being in school all day, or downtown on weekends, with no way to contact my parents or friends. It's odd to even write about it. I keep expecting to say that the main character can call her cell phone and reach someone immediately, or at least leave a message, but I struggle to accept that was impossible.

Although the murders in the convent were fictional, most of the rules, lifestyle, attitudes, and settings in the story were very real.

ABOUT THE AUTHOR

SUSAN MATTERN spent six years as a nun in the late 1960s in St. Louis and this has formed the background for the new *Who Nun It?* Mystery Series. *Old Habits Die Hard* is the second in the series. A classical musician for most of her life, since retirement, Susan has published two e-books. The first, *Out of the Lion's Den*, won the Writer's Digest Grand Prize in 2024. The second book, *Poverty, Chastity, and Disobedience*, is a memoir about her six years in a Catholic convent.

STUDY GUIDE QUESTIONS:

1. What do you think about allowing priests to marry? Do you believe that it would help alleviate the shortage of priests in this country? The Catholic Church trails behind Protestant and Jewish congregations in this respect, particularly when women could fulfill a much-needed role in the church. There is a significant lack of priests, especially in this country, and that role could be addressed by permitting priests to marry and allowing women to become priests. Do you agree or disagree with that?

2. The racial aspect of Kristen and Michael's friendship is mentioned only briefly in the story, but in the late 1960s in the Midwest, it was likely very challenging to be black, or Negro, the term used at the time. The Civil Rights Act had been passed by Congress in 1964, just a few years before the stories take place, and society took a long time to catch up. Do you think we've made significant progress, or that we still have a long way to go in achieving equality? Do you think things are getting worse?

3. Do you believe that honesty is one of the most important factors in a good relationship? Do you think David was justified in becoming so angry with Kristen for lying to him, especially considering she did it with such good intentions? What would you have done in a similar situation? Do you think David would have realized he made a mistake, or would it have marked the end of the relationship?

4. One of the revelations I had while writing the book was the constant reminder of how connected we are today through our cell phones. I had to keep reminding myself that it was

nearly impossible to stay in touch with others as we do now. In the past, you had to go to a phone booth or wait until you reached a location to call someone and let them know where you were. In the convent, choir loft, vineyard, or almost anywhere, you were cut off from communication with others. Moreover, in the convents, we had only one or two phones for the entire house—no private lines—making it even more difficult to have a private conversation with anyone. What an incredible change it is to have cell phones, texting, WhatsApp, and all the various means of communicating. Do you think that constant communication has helped us be closer to each other? I've read a lot about the epidemic of loneliness in our country, even though we have instant communication available. Why do you think that is?

5. Kristen and David have come this far in their relationship, but many problems still exist. There is still a trust issue, the question of children remains unresolved, and Kristen seems uncertain about what love truly means due to her attraction to Michael. Do you think that will pose a stumbling block in their future relationship? Do you think they will stay together? Should they remain together?

6. How has Kristen matured throughout the two books? In what areas does she still exhibit immaturity? What about David? Has he gained any insights regarding his personality and trust issues with Kristen?

Sibylline Press is proud to publish the brilliant work of women authors over 50. We are a woman-owned publishing company and, like our authors, represent women of a certain age.